Alloran's Choice

the andalite chronicles

Look for other 

titles by K.A. Applegate:

#1 The Invasion
#2 The Visitor
#3 The Encounter
#4 The Message
#5 The Predator
#6 The Capture
#7 The Stranger
#8 The Alien
#9 The Secret
#10 The Android
#11 The Forgotten
#12 The Reaction
#13 The Change

<MEGAMORPHS>
#1 The Andalite's Gift

THE ANDALITE CHRONICLES
#1 Elfangor's Journey
#3 An Alien Dies

K.A. Applegate

SCHOLASTIC INC.
New York Toronto London Auckland Sydney

ISBN 0-590-10880-8

12 11 10 9 8 7 6 5 4 3 2 7 8 9/9 0 1 2/0

Printed in the U.S.A. 40

First Scholastic printing, October 1997

For Michael

Prologue

My name is Elfangor.

I am an Andalite prince. And I am about to die.

My fighter is damaged. I have crash-landed on the surface of the planet called Earth. I believe that my great Dome ship has been destroyed. I fear that my little brother Aximili is already dead.

We did not expect the Yeerks to be here in such force. We made a mistake. We underestimated the Yeerks. Not for the first time. We would have defeated their Pool ship and its fighters. But there was a Blade ship in orbit as well.

The Blade ship of Visser Three.

Two Yeerk Bug fighters are landing on either side of me now. The abomination Visser Three is here as well. I can feel him. I can sense his evil.

I cannot defeat the Visser in one-on-one combat. I am weak from my injuries. Too weak to morph. Too weak to fight.

This is my *hirac delest* — my final statement. I have formed the mental link to the thought-speak transponder in my fighter's computer. I will record my memories before the Yeerks annihilate all trace of me.

If this message someday reaches the Andalite world, I want the truth to be known. I am called a great warrior. A hero. But there is a great deal that no Andalite knows about me. I have not lied, but I have kept the truth a secret.

This is not my first visit to Earth. I spent many years on Earth . . . and yet, no time at all.

I landed here now in this construction site because I was looking for a great weapon: the Time Matrix. The existence of this weapon is also a secret.

So many secrets in my life . . . mistakes. Things I should have done. All the strands of my strange life seem to be coming together. It all seems inevitable now. Of course my death would come on Earth. Of course the child would be here. Of course it would be Visser Three who would take my life.

I am too weak to locate the Time ship now. I will die here. But I have left a legacy. Visser Three thinks he has won our long, private war. But I've left a little surprise behind.

I have given the morphing power to five human youths.

I know that in doing this I have broken Andalite law. I know that this action will be condemned by all my people. But the Yeerks are here on Earth. Visser Three is here. The humans must be given a chance to resist. The human race cannot fall to the Yeerks the way the Hork-Bajir race did.

I have given the morphing power to five young humans. Children, really. But sometimes children can accomplish amazing things.

I have no choice but to hope. Because it was I who created Visser Three. I who caused the abomination. I cannot go peacefully to my death, knowing that I created the creature who will enslave the human race.

I came to this place, this empty construction site, looking for the weapon I know is hidden here. But there is no time now. No time . . .

The Visser is here. He is laughing at my weakness. He is savoring his victory over me.

This is the *hirac delest* of Elfangor-Sirinial-Shamtul, Andalite prince. I open my mind in the ritual of death. I open my mind and let all my memories — all my secrets — go to be recorded by the computer.

This is not just a message to my own people. I hope that someday humans will read it as well. Because humans are also my people. Loren . . . and the boy I have just met, but not for the first time. . . .

Alloran's Choice

chapter 1

It was an impossible situation.

I was alone. Alone on an alien planet. Scared, sick at hearts, and overwhelmed.

I flew high above the scene, floating on my six pairs of wings. I was in morph. A four-legged, two-armed Andalite transformed into a twelve-winged *kafit* bird.

Below me was the horizon-to-horizon expanse of the spaceport on the Taxxon home world. Huge, weirdly shaped metal cradles nestled a stunning array of spacecraft. Craft from every corner of the ever-expanding Yeerk Empire: transports and fighters and even a vast Yeerk Pool ship, sitting like a bloated, three-legged spider.

Half a mile to my left was the Skrit Na transport we had chased to the Taxxon world. Inside that ship, unknown to the Yeerks, was the Time Matrix.

Half a mile to my right was the Yeerk transport ship we had seized in orbit. It was loaded to the brim with Yeerks in their natural sluglike bodies. Big, round tubs of Yeerk slugs. Yeerks I had saved when Alloran ordered them destroyed.

And right below me was the *Jahar*. She was like a work of art stuck in a junk pile. She glowed, beautiful amidst the clumsy Yeerk vessels.

And there, stepping from the *Jahar*, were the two odd creatures called humans.

The one called Chapman shoved a helpless, bound Loren. She fell before the feet of Sub-Visser Seven, the Yeerk in charge of security. The sub-visser was a Hork-Bajir-Controller.

"That's what I have to trade," Chapman said. "A whole planet full of . . . *that*."

A hundred Yeerks in different forms — huge, glistening, wormlike Taxxon-Controllers, dangerous, bladed Hork-Bajir-Controllers, clumsy Gedd-Controllers — all stood watching with bated breath.

Where was Arbron, my fellow *aristh*? Where was War-prince Alloran? The last I'd seen of them they were in Taxxon morph. But the two-hour time limit for staying in one morph had passed. I could only hope they had demorphed at some point.

<Alloran should be dealing with all this,> I complained bitterly to no one. Alloran was the war-prince. He'd been in wars before. He had fought in the Hork-Bajir war. I didn't know anything! I was a nobody!

Okay, Elfangor, calm down and think.

But how could I be calm? The Yeerks were seizing Loren and roughly hustling her away. Chapman was trying to communicate with Sub-Visser Seven.

Then it hit me: Chapman knew! He knew about the Time Matrix! If he found a way to tell the Yeerks, we were all done for.

Okay, okay, so I had to do something. Something. *Something*. But what? What should I do? This was madness! The entire fate of my people rested on me? On *me*?

Priorities. Okay, okay, what was most important?

Rescuing Loren.

No. No, that was absurd. The Time Matrix. Everything came down to the Time Matrix.

Was Chapman going to tell the sub-visser about it? No. It was Chapman's biggest bargaining chip. This human was like a Skrit Na — self-serving, greedy, and very, very strange. The Skrit Na are made up of two races. The Skrit look like huge insects and are somewhat less than intelligent. But the Skrit each eventually weave a cocoon and a year later, out pops a Na. The Na stand on four slender legs, have heads shaped like Andalites, but only possess two eyes. All the Skrit Na care about is owning and possessing things. And it seemed the human Chapman was the very same way. So I truly

I had time, but not much. The sub-visser would be kept busy with Chapman attempting to talk about Earth. Like any Yeerk, Sub-Visser Seven would be fascinated by the possibility of an entire planet of sentient creatures for the Yeerk Empire to enslave.

Think, Elfangor. Think!

I couldn't count on finding Alloran and Arbron. But if they were still alive and free, they would reach the same conclusion I had: Go for the Skrit Na ship and its cargo, the Time Matrix.

I turned in the air and flapped my many wings hard as I headed toward the Skrit Na ship.

Below I saw Hork-Bajir grab Loren and pull her to her feet. They yanked her up by her golden hair and a human cry of pain floated up to me.

Priorities, Elfangor.

<Loren. It's me, Elfangor!> I called down, focusing my thought-speak on her alone.

I saw her jerk and turn her head around the way humans do to see behind them.

<Stop. Don't move! Don't make them mad. Don't worry, I'm using private thought-speak. No one else can hear.>

She stopped twisting around and kept marching forward between her Hork-Bajir captors.

<Tell the Yeerks whatever they want to know. Don't resist. Just one thing: Don't mention the Time

Matrix. If they get that, it's all over. You have to trust me. I will save you.>

Of course, the human Loren couldn't answer. Humans don't have thought-speak. Like most species, they make sounds to communicate. I could only hope she would trust me.

Right. She should trust me. Would I trust some alien who'd landed me in this mess?

I could only hope. She had to keep quiet about the Time Matrix. I knew Chapman would.

I flew hard for the Skrit Na ship. At least I had a goal now. That helped. A little. And I just wouldn't think about the insanity of it all. I would just put all that out of my head.

The Skrit Na ship was being fussed over by Gedd-Controllers. Gedds are clumsy, loping creatures. They were the first species the Yeerks infested. Only low-ranking Yeerks were still stuck in Gedd bodies. These Gedd-Controllers seemed to be busy checking the Skrit Na ship for hull damage.

I had to get aboard that ship. And I had to fly it off the planet.

No problem, Elfangor. Just steal the ship from the middle of a Yeerk spaceport and fly it away without getting zapped. No big deal.

I landed in the dirt beneath the ship's cradle. It was dark and filthy down there. Endless debris and trash had been shoved in over the years. They had apparently even emptied ships' sewage reprocessing plants there. The smell was overwhelming.

I demorphed amid the fossilized remains of sewage from a dozen species. Not pleasant. But it was a good feeling to get my Andalite body back.

I cowered behind the massive support pillars as I watched my four legs grow from four of the *kafit*'s wings. Two other wings became my hands. My sleek bird head grew large and sprouted my twin stalk eyes, while the bird's own two eyes became my main eyes.

The remaining wings shriveled and disappeared as my long, wispy bird tail became my swift, powerful Andalite tail.

I was so pleased to get my tail back. A bird's body can be pretty helpless. But unfortunately, I couldn't stay in Andalite form. An Andalite walking around on the Taxxon world, surrounded by nothing but various types of Yeerks, would be just slightly obvious. Slightly obvious, as in I'd have been dead ten seconds after I walked out of the shadows.

I had only one way to go. I would have to resume the Taxxon morph I had acquired. The Taxxon DNA was still a part of me. It always would be.

I swallowed my fear and loathing and began the morph.

And as I felt the huge worm body grow, and felt the screaming, desperate Taxxon hunger rise within

I swallowed my fear and loathing and began the morph.

And as I felt the huge worm body grow, and felt the screaming, desperate Taxxon hunger rise within me, I tried to form a plan. A plan to save my world, my friends, and Loren all at once.

I was halfway into Taxxon shape when I heard the shuffling, slithering sound of a Taxxon. My stalk eyes had already morphed away. But I still had my main eyes. I turned to look.

It was just a dozen feet away. It must have been lurking in the darkness. It had only to scream for help and I'd be Taxxon lunch.

Then, to my surprise, the Taxxon spoke in Andalite thought-speak.

<Elfangor! Is that you?>

<Arbron?> I cried. I was flooded with relief. I wouldn't be alone! I had Arbron with me. We'd never exactly been close friends, but at least he was one of my own.

<Yes, it's me,> he said.

<What happened to you?> I asked. <I lost you and Alloran in that terrible feeding frenzy.>

For a few moments Arbron said nothing. His silence drew a chill up my half-morphed body.

<I guess we got separated,> Arbron said flatly. <So. We gonna rescue this Time Matrix thing or what? Hero time, huh?>

<I don't know. I lost him in the crowd. Just you and me, I guess. Come on. Let's do it. Let's save the world, hah-hah! Just what you planned, eh, Elfangor? Elfangor the hero?>

He seemed to alternate between being flat and emotionless and sudden bursts of manic energy. Maybe it was the strain. The fear. And the vile creepiness of inhabiting a Taxxon form.

That had to be it. Nothing to worry about. Just stress.

<If I end up being a hero, you'll be one, too,> I said. <Besides, let's just see if we survive first.>

<Yeah. Survive;> he said, flat and emotionless again. <Come on, Elfangor. Finish morphing.>

chapter 2

<You have a plan?>

<Sure,> I said. <We bluff. We tell those Gedd-Controllers up there that we've come to fix the computers. Then we fly that sorry Skrit Na ship away.>

I wanted to sound casual. Nonchalant. The way the fighter pilots always sound when they are describing some terrifying battle. Like it was all no big deal.

Arbron stared at me through red jelly Taxxon eyes. <Okay. Lead the way,> he said.

Arbron and I slithered out from beneath the ship's cradle and motored our rows of Taxxon needle legs up the ramp to the ship itself. Just a pair of bored Taxxon technicians going to work. Totally calm.

Or as calm as any Taxxon, even a Taxxon-Controller, can ever be. There is simply no way to explain the awful hunger of the Taxxon. It is beyond any hunger you've ever imagined. It is constant.

Like a screaming voice in your head. Screaming so loud you can't think.

Every living thing you see or smell is just meat to you. You hear beating hearts and smell rushing blood and the hunger almost takes over your body.

And when someone is injured . . . when there is blood spilled . . . well then, as I knew personally, the hunger is all but impossible to resist.

I had come within a haunch hair of eating an injured Taxxon myself. Not something I wanted to remember. But not something I'd ever forget.

<Don't hesitate,> I advised Arbron as several Gedds turned to blink curiously at us. <Look like you're on your way to work.>

<Shut up, Elfangor,> Arbron said harshly.

Again I felt the chill of fear. Something was horribly wrong. But there was no stopping now. I pushed rudely past a Gedd who was in my way.

The Gedd-Controllers looked resentful. But they had no reason to suspect us. We were Taxxons. They had to assume we were Taxxon-Controllers. We looked like we were there to work. No reason for them to be at all suspicious.

Except that one of them was.

One of the Gedd-Controllers stood right in front of us, seemingly unimpressed. He spoke in *Galard*, the language of interstellar trade. It sounded hard on his Gedd tongue, but I could understand him.

"Rrr-what arrrre you doing herrrrrre?"

If it was hard for the Gedd to make *Galard* sounds, it was almost impossible for me, with a Taxxon's mouth and tongue. But I couldn't use thought-speak. I might as well announce that I was Andalite. I had to try to speak *Galard* with a three-foot-long Taxxon tongue.

So I tried. "Sreeeee snwwweeeyiiir sreeeyah!"

Which was not even close to being the sounds I'd wanted to make. What I had meant to say was "computer repair." But the Taxxon's tongue is so long, that it would be hard even if I was used to using a mouth to make sounds.

The Gedd stared at me with its tiny yellow eyes. "Rrr-use rrr pad!" He pointed furiously down at a small computer pad attached to his wrist.

<It's some kind of translator,> Arbron said. <Some primitive version of our own translator chips. Let me do it.>

He reached with one of his weak, two-fingered Taxxon hands and pressed several buttons. From the pad came a disembodied voice, speaking *Galard*.

"Computer repair."

The Gedd snorted angrily. "Rrryou Taxxon wearrrers think you rrrown the planet! Arrogant as Horrrk-Bajir!"

Arbron and I shoved past him into the Skrit Na

ship. Unfortunately, it was so cramped and low that we could barely drag our massive bodies inside.

The bridge of the Skrit Na ship was identical to the Skrit Na ship we'd boarded to rescue the two humans. There were two cocooned Skrit glued into a corner. They wouldn't cause any trouble. They didn't look ready to hatch into Na just yet. And there was an active Skrit, what Loren had described as a giant cockroach, scurrying around almost brainlessly, polishing and cleaning.

There were no Na that I could see. Aside from the Skrit, the bridge of the ship was empty.

<So far, so good,> I muttered. <I'm going to close the hatch. We'll demorph, power up, and be off-planet before they know what's hit them.>

<Yeah. Okay,> Arbron said. <Ready?>

<Yep.> I focused on my breathing, trying to fight the raging Taxxon hunger and my own fear. <Okay, do it!>

Arbron punched the pad to close the hatch door. It slid shut and made a snug vacuum seal SHWOOMP!

I focused all my thoughts on demorphing. I wanted out of that Taxxon body. The two of us could barely move in the cramped bridge, let alone fly the ship. The idiot Skrit kept banging against me, unable to find a way to go around.

I demorphed. I shed that vile Taxxon body as fast

as I could. I felt the awful hunger weaken and my own Andalite mind rise above, freed of the Taxxon's instincts.

THUMP! THUMP! THUMP!

The Gedds were pounding on the hull. "Rrrrwhat arrrre you doing? Open rrrup!"

I ignored the noise and punched the engine power. The main engines began to whine as they powered up.

And then I realized it. Arbron was not demorphing.

<Arbron, what are you waiting for? Demorph!>

Arbron didn't say anything.

THUMP! THUMP! THUMP!

"Rrrr-open up! Powerrr down rrryou fool!"

<Arbron! What are you up to? Demorph!> I yelled. I guess I hoped that yelling would make it happen. But I already knew. He stared at me through those shimmering red jelly eyes, and I knew. More quietly, almost begging, I said, <Come on, Arbron. Demorph.>

<I really wish I could, Elfangor,> he said. <I really wish I could.>

chapter 3

There was no time to talk about it. We had to get the Skrit Na ship up and out of that cradle before it occurred to the Yeerks that we were stealing it.

No time to talk about it. But time to feel something of the terror Arbron felt.

I had been in Taxxon morph. I had felt the hunger. I'd rather be dead than be trapped in that body forever.

Arbron's weak Taxxon "arms" pushed all the right buttons, and I felt the soft vibration of the engines reaching full power.

The Gedd-Controllers outside must have felt it, too. Suddenly they stopped pounding on the ship. They were probably running for dear life. The radiation blast of the engines would be captured and contained within the cradle. But if you were still hanging around on that cradle when the engines came on, you wouldn't last long.

<Ready?> I asked Arbron.

<Ready.>

<Then hang on, because I don't know how much of a kick these Skrit Na ships have.> I punched up a burn and we rose from the pad.

Unfortunately, we didn't rise very quickly.

<What is the matter with this thing?> I yelled. I looked at the air speed indicator. We were doing a bare thousand miles per hour. And the acceleration rate was way too slow.

<It'll take us ten minutes just to get escape velocity!> Arbron cried.

<Yeerk ships will be all over us before we can even think about going to Zero-space,> I said.

<The Time Matrix!> Arbron said. <We can use it! We can escape through time!>

<No! We don't know how fast it works. If we try to activate the Time Matrix, the power signature will light up every Yeerk sensor within a million miles! What if it takes ten minutes for *it* to work? Besides . . . we don't know who else might get mad if you use that thing.>

<What? You're worried about what some prince will say if we survive?>

<No. I'm not worried about our superiors. Or at least, I figure my career in the military is already destroyed.>

<Then what are you . . . > Arbron fell silent. Then he laughed. <Are you kidding me? You're worried about some mythical Ellimists?>

<Mythical? That's what some people used to say about the Time Matrix itself. Someone built that machine. Who else, if not the Ellimists? And do we want to take the chance of making them angry?>

I felt a little foolish. My parents had told me Ellimist stories when I was a child. Stories of the all-powerful, inexplicable creatures who sometimes interfered in the affairs of simpler species. I halfway expected a snide remark from Arbron.

But Arbron didn't answer. He was staring at his display board. At least, I guess he was staring. Taxxon eyes don't exactly focus normally. <Yeerk patrol ship coming up on an intercept vector! It's a Bug fighter!>

<Can we take on a Bug fighter?>

<Are you kidding? All the Skrit Na ever have are secondhand, low-power Dracon beams the Yeerks sell off for scrap. That Bug fighter has twin Penetrator-Class Dracon beams. We can't trade shots with them!>

He was right. And I should have remembered that. But I was shaken. Confused. My brain was spinning at a million revolutions per second and going nowhere.

I had to think. Focus.

The air speed gauge now showed two thousand twenty miles per hour. The hull was blistering hot from the air resistance. <Wait a minute! Bug fighters

are slow in atmosphere, right? They can't handle the heat. We can! So far, at least. We're doing better than two thousand miles per hour. We're faster than they are in atmosphere!>

<You're going to try and outrun them in the atmosphere?>

<You have a better option?>

<We have a second Bug fighter on us!> Arbron answered. <Two more launching!>

<We're going to the grass,> I said, hoping I sounded more confident than I felt. <I'll need direct vision. Real time, real aspect. Open a window.>

Arbron played his console, and suddenly the panel in front of me became a window. I could see the superheated air, blazing around the ship.

I nosed the stubby, round ship down. As we dropped we picked up speed. <Passing three thousand miles per hour!>

Down, down, down at over three thousand mph! The brown dust of the Taxxon world leaped up at us.

Spacecraft are designed for the almost total vacuum of space. Usually they are barely functional in atmosphere. But the Skrit Na were scavengers who went from planet to planet, kidnapping and stealing and performing their inexplicable medical experiments. So they needed ships that could handle atmosphere.

But nothing is really designed to do three thousand miles an hour in atmosphere. Let alone fifty feet off the ground.

We had been seven miles up, right at the outer edge of the Taxxon atmosphere. We dropped back down to ground level in five point eight seconds.

<Yaaaaahhhhh!>

<Yaaaaahhhhh!>

We both screamed in a mix of utter terror and shocking excitement. Let me tell you something: Millions of miles an hour in empty space is *nothing* compared to three thousand miles an hour going straight for the ground.

<Pull up! Pull up! Pull up!>

I pulled up, as the collision warnings screamed in the Skrit Na language.

We blew across the Taxxon desert, trailing sonic booms that must have sounded like nuclear explosions going off in our wake.

<Can you get the Bug fighters on visual?> I asked.

<On screen!>

I saw two Bug fighters racing after us, one behind the other. Their hulls glowed bright with friction heat. But they weren't backing off.

<Fine,> I muttered. <Let's see who's faster.> I raised the burn and felt a slight lurch as the engines pushed harder still.

<Three thousand two hundred miles per hour,> Arbron reported. <Three point three K. Three point four K. Hull temperature is . . . you don't even want to know. Three point five K.>

Three thousand five hundred miles an hour. The ground was a blur. We were a blazing meteorite. We were an arrow of flame as we shot across the Taxxon world at impossible speeds. The scruffy bushes and stunted trees of the Taxxon world burst into flame as we passed over. We were drawing a line of fire around the planet!

<Pull up!> Arbron yelled.

Mountains rose up like a wall. <Where did *they* come from?!> I cried as I pulled up, straining every atom in the Skrit Na ship.

The ship bucked like a dying beast in its final agony. But we climbed. Up . . . up . . .

<Are we going to clear?>

Before I could answer, we shot over the mountain wall. I swear I heard the bottom scrape as we cleared the height.

Unfortunately, the Yeerks knew the local topography. They'd been ready for them. They had adjusted easily and had gained on us.

TSSSSEEEEWWWW!

A red Dracon beam lanced past us, missing by inches. They were close enough now to shoot.

We were approaching the dividing line between night and day. I could see it rushing toward me.

Suddenly, out of the corner of my eye, I saw the lead Bug fighter simply explode! The air friction had finally worn down its compensators and the craft had burned to a cinder in a split second.

<Yah-hah! One Yeerk fried!> I exulted.

<Elfangor, we're next if we don't slow down,> Arbron warned.

<There are still three Bug fighters on our tail,> I said.

<We are about five minutes away from burning up,> Arbron said. <Can you guarantee those Bug fighters will cinder before we do?>

<What do you have in mind?>

<We take a shot. One, two, three. They won't be ready. They won't expect it.>

I turned my stalk eyes to stare at Arbron. <No one can make that shot.>

<I can,> he said.

<With Taxxon eyes?> I didn't want to throw that in his face, but I had to be realistic. <With Taxxon reaction times? With Skrit Na targeting computers?>

<I can make the shot, Elfangor,> he said calmly.

<Look, Arbron, I want to come out of this alive.>

<And you think I don't care if I live or die, right?> he said bitterly. <Maybe you're right. This

hunger . . . Elfangor, you've felt it. You know. But I can still make this shot.>

<You always laugh at *me* wanting to be a hero,> I said. <Now who's playing hero?>

He didn't answer.

I looked at the hull temperature readout. He was right. We would cinder in a few minutes.

You know what's funny? I wanted to ask the captain what to do. It seemed ridiculous that I should make a life and death decision like this. Princes made those kinds of decisions. Captains made those decisions.

Only I *was* the captain. And if I was wrong, we would dig a hole in the Taxxon dirt at three thousand miles an hour.

<Okay, Arbron,> I said. <In ten seconds. Ten . . . nine . . . eight . . . >

chapter 4

<Three . . . two . . .>

I killed thrust and punched the air brakes.

SHHHHHRRRRREEEEEEEKKKK!

The Skrit Na ship shook; it bucked; it rattled; it vibrated; it bounced wildly just fifty feet off the grass.

I was thrown off-balance. I sprawled across the deck. But Arbron's rows of Taxxon legs absorbed the punishment. He never wavered. He kept his Taxxon claws on the targeting controls.

Our speed dropped from nearly three and a half thousand miles per hour down to half that. In mere seconds! Too fast for the Bug fighters to react.

What happened next would make Arbron a hero.

Our speed dropped off; the Bug fighters rocketed forward and blew past, doing fifteen hundred mph faster than us.

Arbron fired! TSSSEEEEEWWW!

Fired! TSSSEEEEEWWW!

Fired! TSSSEEEEEWWW!

Three shots at three targets doing a relative speed of fifteen hundred mph. Three shots in atmosphere! Three shots from a vibrating, bucking wreck of a Skrit Na ship.

I dragged myself up and stared in disbelief out of the forward window.

Three spinning meteorites, three balls of flame, slammed into the ground. They dug craters in the Taxxon dirt and extinguished themselves.

<Nice shooting!> I said. <Seriously nice shooting!>

<Thanks. It turns out Taxxon senses and reflexes are good at this kind of thing. Guess that's why the Yeerks use Taxxon-Controllers to fly their Bug fighters. It's nice to know there's something useful about this disgusting body.>

<We're going to find a way to get you out of that Taxxon morph,> I said. I tried to sound like I meant it. What else could I say?

Till that moment I'd been too busy trying to stay alive to really think about what had happened to Arbron. Maybe we'd never exactly been best friends, but it was still horrible to look at his foul Taxxon body and think that this was how he would remain. To look into those emotionless red jelly eyes and realize that he was in there, looking back at me.

And I knew what he was feeling, now that the

battle was done. The terror. The despair. The awful Taxxon hunger.

I turned the Skrit Na ship around and headed back toward the rushing line of daylight.

<What are you doing?> Arbron demanded.

<I need a place to land and conceal this ship,> I said. <I need daylight. And I need to be closer to the spaceport. We can't just leave the others behind.>

<Others? You mean Alloran?>

<And the humans,> I said. <They are our responsibility.>

<We are not going back to the spaceport,> Arbron said. <The Yeerks are back there. And Taxxons. They'll catch us. Do you know what they'll do if they catch me? They'll eat me alive, Elfangor.>

<Arbron, you have to hold on. You have to try and hold on.> We were racing back across the dark mountains. Back toward the retreating line of daylight.

<Hold on? Hold on? Are you insane? If we go back there, they'll eat me! Turn this ship back. I'm going to use the Time Matrix! I'm going back in time. I'm going back to my life!>

<You can't light up that Time Matrix. The power signature will be visible to every ship in orbit, every satellite, every —>

<I don't care! I don't care if I die, just let this

hunger stop. Stop it. Stop it. Stop it! You fool, don't you know I could eat you right now?>

I turned my main eyes toward Arbron. I knew that inside there was a scared Andalite *aristh*. But what I actually saw was the nightmare worm. What I saw was the sloppy red eyes, the round, gasping, eternally hungry mouth.

For a moment that seemed to stretch and stretch, we stared at each other. I don't know what was going through Arbron's mind right then. I don't know what conclusions he'd reached. I only know what he did.

"Sssrrrreeeeyyyyyaaahhh!" he screamed in his slithering, high-pitched Taxxon voice. He reared back, practically laying the upper third of his body horizontal. And then he slammed down on me.

Slammed his upper body down, red mouth open wide.

I could have killed him. He knew that, of course. He knew that no Taxxon could hope to outfight an Andalite. But I could not kill him. Not even if that's what he wanted.

I dodged to my right.

He slammed hard into the instrument panel. Sparks erupted!

He swept his upper body toward me, hoping to slam me against the bulkhead and stun me.

I leaped inside his reach and struck!

SLASH! Two of his needle legs went rolling across the floor.

SLASH! And two more legs were gone.

Arbron sagged. The front part of his body could no longer be held up. He lay, fully prone, a huge, helpless worm.

<Just kill me!> he screamed.

But I was busy. The control panel had been half-wrecked. The ship was bucking and yawing. It was unstable. I reduced power. We had shot across the line into twilight. But I couldn't see into the deep shadows between the mountain peaks.

<You can't leave me like this!> Arbron cried.

<I'm going to get you help,> I yelled. <But I have to land this ship!>

<Elfangor! You know what happens to wounded Taxxons! You *know*!>

<I'll protect you,> I cried desperately as the ship bucked and shook harder and harder. The two cocooned Skrit seemed about to break loose from their moorings. The active Skrit had gone to the cargo hold. Maybe, even as unintelligent as the Skrit are, he knew better than to be anywhere near a hungry Taxxon.

<You can't protect me. Fool! Nothing can stop them! Nothing can stop the hunger. I couldn't stop it. Alloran couldn't stop it. Don't you understand? I

ate, Elfangor. I ate that wounded Taxxon. I couldn't help myself!>

<Shut up!> I screamed. <Shut up!>

I didn't want to hear anymore. I couldn't. I had to focus. I had to land the ship or we'd both die. I had to shut Arbron up.

I swept my stalk eyes around the bridge. Where would the Skrit Na keep weapons? There. A green panel marked with Skrit Na script.

I stretched my left arm to reach the panel. Popped it open. Yes. A handheld Dracon beam. Old and dusty and probably badly maintained, like most Skrit Na things.

I found the power setting. I set it at the lowest intensity.

<What are you doing?> Arbron yelled.

<I have to land this ship, Arbron. Keep quiet or I'll stun you.>

<If you fire that thing, you'll kill me,> Arbron said. <You have the settings backward. That's originally a Yeerk weapon. Setting one is the highest setting, not the lowest.>

Suddenly, I knew what Arbron would do. He couldn't rise up, but he could still scuttle forward. He came straight for me, rushing and slithering, as if he were aiming his round red mouth at me.

He was trying to force me to shoot him. To shoot him with the Dracon beam set on maximum! But

I was too fast for him. I twisted the dial to ten. I fired.

And just as my finger was tightening on the trigger . . . I realized Arbron had outsmarted me. He'd lied, and I'd fallen for it. Arbron had always been a better student than me. He was a qualified exodatologist. He knew alien systems far better than me.

I tried to stop. But my finger squeezed. The Dracon beam fired. On *maximum* power.

But by chance, or maybe by some desperate, too-late twitch of my finger, the beam missed Arbron by a millimeter.

Instead, it blew a two-foot hole through the hull of the ship.

After that, everything was noise and spinning and pain and confusion.

chapter 5

I woke up.

I was on my side, lying in the dirt.

I looked up at a night sky. Stars, galaxies, three tiny moons.

Where was I?

I stood up. Every muscle in my body ached. Muscles I didn't even know I had ached. My hooves tasted nothing but bare dirt. My stalk eyes swiveled quickly to look around, but I realized one eye was blinded.

Then I saw the ship, the Skrit Na transport. It was still more or less in one piece. I must have been able to land it. Somehow. I couldn't remember much of those last few minutes. It was all chaos in my brain.

I forced myself to go over the facts. I was on the Taxxon home world. I was approximately four hundred miles from the spaceport. Loren and Chapman were in the hands of the Yeerks. Alloran . . . no one knew.

Arbron had tried to trick me into killing him. That's what I remembered best.

<Arbron!> I called. <Arbron!>

No answer. I trudged wearily over to the Skrit Na ship. I saw the two-foot hole made by the Dracon beam. And then I saw the way the engines had been ripped half off. The ship would never fly again.

I climbed into the wreckage. My second stalk eye was starting to clear a little. I felt it and realized it had just been covered with mud.

Inside the ship I called again. <Arbron!> I looked around. Nothing was working except a tiny glimmer of emergency lighting. For some reason the Skrit Na liked their emergency lighting to be green. Who knows why?

Something was missing.

Of course! The two Skrit cocoons. They must have been knocked loose.

The door to the freight hold was blown open. I went in. The same green emergency lighting illuminated a bizarre scene. In the hold were boxes and crates piled in wild disarray. Many had broken open on impact. They spilled an amazing mass of alien-looking objects. Frozen, preserved animals; bundles of the artificial skin that Loren and Chapman wore; glass objects that seemed to contain liquids; odd, antiquated electronic equipment; small objects that looked like hundreds of rectangular sheets of paper glued together on one side; and a long crate of what I could almost swear were primitive weapons.

All things that the Skrit Na had looted from Earth. Loren would know what they were, no doubt.

But in addition to all the small objects, there were two much larger things. One was a shiny yellow-painted creation with four black wheels.

The other object was the most powerful thing in the history of the galaxy.

It looked like nothing more than a smooth, off-white sphere. It was perhaps ten feet in diameter. Perfectly smooth. Unmarked. You would never know what it was if you hadn't seen the power readings. Invisible to the eye, it spread its grid down through the very fabric of time-space.

The Time Matrix.

I found I had stopped breathing. I could barely imagine the power I was staring at. To move a ship into Zero-space took more power than a medium-sized star. To move anything through time took ten times that power. The power of ten suns. All somehow contained in that off-white sphere.

<Arbron!> I yelled.

But I knew he wasn't there. He must have been thrown clear of the ship, just as I had been. Only I hadn't seen him outside. And now it occurred to me that something else was missing, too. The active Skrit.

Both Skrit cocoons and the active Skrit were gone. Along with Arbron.

I turned slowly away from the Time Matrix. It had a hold over me. It drew my stalk eyes back to it, even as I walked away.

I went back outside. <Arbron!>

The light of the moons and stars was too dim to see clearly. But I had the impression I was in a narrow valley between tall, almost clifflike mountains. Where could Arbron have gotten to? Had he fallen from the doomed Skrit Na ship earlier? He could have ended up slamming into one of the mountainsides.

I hated to even imagine that.

I went back inside the cargo hold and picked up a handful of paper sheaves. Some were larger and had pictures. By the dim green light I instantly recognized that the pictures were of humans.

I flipped through pictures of humans doing things I could not understand. But then there was one picture I understood immediately. It showed a marvelously tall waterfall. The waterfall crashed into a pool surrounded by trees, all of them green. Overhead was a blue sky.

Two humans were smiling and sticking tiny white cylinders into their mouths.

There was human writing beneath the picture. I don't read human very well. But I was sure it was a poem to the beauty revealed in the picture.

The grass there looked sweet.

It would be a fine thing to run there. To run with Loren and forget everything that had happened. Forget that I was alone on a planet of evil, my only companion probably dead, my prince lost.

I turned to other pictures. I saw small, strange pictures of humans doing nothing but smiling. And there were pictures of human technology. A flying machine of some sort. Humans holding long rods that spit fire. What seemed to be hideous cities. And then, to my delight, a picture of an actual human spacecraft.

It took me a few seconds to understand what it was. It seemed to be a chemical rocket. An actual chemical rocket!

But the pictures that drew my gaze were the ones of beautiful beaches beside blue seas. And mountains topped with white. And rushing white-water streams surrounded by tall green trees.

The trees were all very similar. Not as beautiful as the trees I knew. Still, the pictures spoke of a lovely world, filled with delicious green grass and cool water.

That alien landscape of Earth took me away from the drab horror of the Taxxon world. I wondered if Chapman might be from the jagged human cities. Was that why he was so much harsher than Loren? Was Loren from the beautiful green country where smiling humans stuck white cylinders in their mouths?

I guess I fell asleep looking at that picture. I awoke with lingering traces of awful dreams chasing through my brain.

There was light . . . natural light from the Taxxon sun.

I ran outside. As I had guessed, I was in an incredibly steep valley. And now I could see tracks in the orange dirt. The marks of dozens of needle-sharp legs. Taxxon tracks!

The tracks came right up to the ship. Had they come while I was asleep? No. I could see my own tracks from the night before. My tracks were over the Taxxon tracks.

Arbron! They were his tracks. Had to be. And yet . . . No, there had been more than one Taxxon. Three . . . four others. Five sets altogether.

And then I saw two additional signs. A set of wandering, insectlike tracks, and the evidence of something large being dragged away.

<The Skrit,> I said. <Okay. So Taxxons came. They took Arbron away. And the Skrit. And maybe the two cocooned Skrit.>

I glanced at the spot where I'd been lying unconscious. They had to have seen me, smelled me. And yet I was still alive.

<They have Arbron,> I realized.

I reeled back and fell down. The Taxxons had taken Arbron. I knew what Taxxons did with prisoners.

<No!> What had I done? I'd let them take Arbron alive!

And yet why hadn't they taken me? And the Time Matrix? Surely Taxxon-Controllers would not have done that.

I recalled Sub-Visser Seven's reference to Mountain Taxxons — Taxxons who refused to submit to Yeerk control. And I felt just the faintest glimmer of hope. If these had been Yeerk-controlled Taxxons, they'd have taken the Time Matrix. And me.

<What am I supposed to do now?> I asked the empty, dusty sky.

Should I try to follow the tracks to Arbron? No. I had to be logical. Whatever type of Taxxon he'd fallen in with, their hunger would almost certainly seal his doom. And the doom of the poor Skrit Na, too.

Alloran might still be alive. He was my prince. My duty was to get back to him. Tell him about the Time Matrix and Arbron. Somehow. But the Taxxon spaceport was hundreds of miles away, across burning sands.

Then . . . one of the human pictures I'd seen came back to me. It had shown two smiling humans sitting in something very much like the bright yellow machine in the cargo hold.

I went back to the ship. Yes, this bright yellow machine had four wheels. And you could easily see how humans might sit in it. It had a name in chrome letters: "Mustang." Naturally, I had no idea what that meant.

I set to work enlarging the hole in the side of the cargo hold. Then I removed the chairs in the machine. I discovered that I could fit inside the machine if I removed the flimsy cloth top. I stared long and hard at the control panel. The computer was tiny and had knobs you could twist. But at first all it did was make static noises.

Then I discovered an actual tape drive! Astoundingly primitive. I pushed the buttons on the small keypad and twisted the knobs again, and to my utter amazement, the computer began to play music.

"I can't get no . . . satisfaction!" it screamed.

I quickly turned it down. What kind of race would use a computer to play screaming sounds?

It took twenty minutes more for me to realize that a notched brass insert could be twisted. And when I twisted it . . .

RRRR RRRRR RRRRRRRR PUH PUH PUH VROOOOM!

The noise was amazing!

It was an actual chemical engine! Something from a thousand years ago! Ridiculously primitive, and yet I found when I pressed my forehoof on a pedal in the floor, the engine roared.

VVVRRRRROOOOM! VVVRROOOOOM! VVVROOOOOOM!

It was primitive, all right. But it vibrated in a most satisfying way. And I liked it.

chapter 6

I have run mag-hover trucks.

I have flown Bug fighters.

I have flown Skrit Na raiders at three thousand miles per hour *in atmosphere*.

But I had never experienced anything more exhilarating than racing down the valley and out across the open Taxxon desert in my Mustang. It only went a hundred miles per hour, but with the wind in your face, whipping your fur, bending your stalk eyes back, it was certainly a wild ride.

But everything was going wrong.

I was racing across the Taxxon desert in a human vehicle toward probable doom. But with the wind in my face, and the music in my ears mingling with the loud roar of the engine, I didn't feel so badly.

I had gathered up some of the other human objects the Skrit Na had taken. The writing sheets with pictures. Some of the machines that looked like weapons. And some of the glass bottles containing liquid.

I broke several of the bottles before I figured out

how to open them. After that, I quickly determined that they contained water-based liquids. I poured the liquids into a shallow pan, and was able to stick in one hoof to drink as I drove.

DR. PEPPER, the bottles had said. I figured that was human writing for "bubbling brown water."

For a while I just put Arbron out of my mind. I put Alloran out of my mind. And I pictured myself with Loren, driving in my Mustang across the green grass of Earth. Wind in my face. Bubbling brown water running up my hoof.

As I drove, I tried to come up with a plan. One thing was for sure: An Andalite in a Mustang was going to be just slightly obvious. I would need stealth. But I would not morph to Taxxon again.

Not ever.

That's when the ground beneath my wheels simply opened up.

FFFFWWWUUUMMPPP!

<Aaaaahhhh!>

BOOM! BOOM! RUMBLERUMBLERUMBLE!

The Mustang tumbled and rattled down a steep, rough slope. A dirt ramp that led straight down into darkness.

<Aaaaahhhh!>

I took my hoof off the accelerator pedal. I tried to reach the key to turn off the engine. But the vibration was too severe.

I slid and rattled and rolled in my human machine, down, down, down into the ground. Down and down. And then I slid to a halt.

SCRRUUMMPPFFF!

The only sound was the noise of the engine and the weird human moaning that passed for music.

". . . gimme, gimme, gimme the honky-tonk blues!"

I turned off the music.

I was in darkness, but not the absolute darkness I expected. This darkness still afforded sight. There was light enough for my main eyes to see, after they'd had a few seconds to adjust.

I was in a vast underground cavern. Dominating the center of the cavern was a sort of hill or small mountain. It was this mountain that glowed. It glowed a dim but unmistakable red.

From this irregular glowing hill came tendrils, each perhaps three or four feet in diameter. As my eyes adjusted I could see that there were a dozen or more of these tendrils, and that each one extended to the edge of the cavern and then kept going into the rock itself.

The tendrils, too, glowed a dim red. I realized that I could see things moving inside the tendrils. The tendrils were hollow! They were tubes, each about as big around as . . .

As a Taxxon!

I saw them then. My eyes finally pierced the darkness and saw the Taxxons! Dozens . . . no, hundreds! They swarmed around and over the glowing red mountain.

As I watched, I saw holes open in the sides of the tunnel-tendrils. Out crawled more Taxxons.

They had to see me. They couldn't help but see me. And yet none moved to attack me.

Instead, they busied themselves pushing dirt and rock back into place to fill the space my Mustang had created.

<IS THIS THE CREATURE?>

<Aaaarrrrggghh!> I screamed.

The voice in my head was huge! Massive! I grabbed my head with my hands. It was like hearing a planet speak! It was only then, as I staggered under the psychic blow, that I realized it: The red mountain was alive!

I heard a different thought-speak voice. <Yes. That's him,> Arbron said. <He is called Elfangor.>

One Taxxon came slithering toward me out of the mass of bodies around the base of the red mountain. It moved clumsily. Two rows of legs were shorter than the others.

<Arbron?>

<Yes, Elfangor. It's me.>

<I was afraid you were dead,> I said.

<I wanted to be. But I am still alive. Alive to serve the Living Hive.>

<The what?>

He waved one Taxxon claw back toward the massive, glowing mountain. <The Living Hive. Light of the Taxxons. Mother and Father of the Taxxons. The Hive has lost many of its children to the Yeerks. Many of its servants have betrayed the Hive and made an alliance with the Yeerks. But the Living Hive is still the Mother and Father of the species.>

<Arbron, what are you talking about? Have they done something to you?>

Then he laughed — the old Arbron again, for just a moment. <Have they done something to me? Well, they didn't eat me, if that's what you mean. The Taxxons who found us after we crashed wanted to eat us both. But I gave them the Skrit instead. I had no choice! And then the Living Hive learned what I was. It drew me here.>

<We're hundreds of miles from where we landed. How did you get here? You couldn't possibly have walked.>

<The Living Hive's tunnels extend across thousands of miles, Elfangor. There is suction in the tunnels. A Taxxon has only to fold back its legs, and the pressure draws it swiftly down the tunnel, as the Hive commands.>

<The legs I . . . the legs you were missing. They're growing back.>

<Yes. Taxxons can regenerate legs.>

<Arbron . . . what's going on? It wasn't an accident that the ground opened up beneath me. Did the . . . the Living Hive want me here for some reason?>

<Yes, Elfangor. The Hive is angry.>

<At me?> I asked, feeling my guts turn over several times. If this glowing red mountain was mad at me, all it had to do was yell in its monstrous psychic voice and I'd be shattered.

<The Living Hive is tired of losing its children to the Yeerks. The Living Hive has long sought a way to destroy the Yeerk invaders and remove them from this planet. But the Hive could not understand the Yeerks and their machines. Now . . . now, the Hive has an adviser. Someone who understands machines, spaceships, Dracon beams. Someone who will help the Hive destroy the Yeerks and their traitor Taxxons.>

I stared at Arbron. <You?>

He laughed. But this time there was no mirth. <What better future could I have, Elfangor? I am Taxxon now. And now I am preparing for a surprise attack on the spaceport. The Hive will send a thousand of her children with me. I will lead a Taxxon rebellion.>

I didn't say anything. What was there to say? My hearts were breaking.

Arbron slithered closer, shuffling on his needle-like legs. He looked at me through red jelly eyes. And even now, I knew he seethed with raging Taxxon hunger.

<Don't pity me, Elfangor. I am glad I didn't die. Any life is better than none. And no matter how awful things seem, there is always meaning and purpose to be found.>

<And you've found your purpose?>

<We attack tonight. The Living Hive is pushing her tunnels closer to the spaceport. A thousand Taxxons will pour from the ground, surprising the Yeerks and all their creatures.>

I imagined that moment. A thousand huge, hungry worms, erupting amid the technological cathedrals of the ship's cradles. Erupting amidst Taxxon-Controllers and Hork-Bajir-Controllers.

<You'll lose,> I said.

<We know,> Arbron said. <But even a Taxxon has the right to control its own planet. Even a Taxxon has the right to resist an invader.>

<But you can't win,> I said flatly.

<Aren't lost causes sometimes the best causes, Elfangor?>

How could he imagine that anything to do with Taxxons could ever be a good cause? These Taxxons were no less cannibalistic. No less murderous. And yet, if they opposed the Yeerks, could I refuse to offer that help?

<Tell me what I can do to help, Arbron.>

<That's more like it, Elfangor. We'll put some tail blades into these Yeerks, right? Right? We'll be heroes, after all.>

chapter 7

All that afternoon I stayed in the horrible, reeking, stifling darkness of that underground cavern. Arbron was there some of the time. But not often. Mostly he was communing with the Living Hive. Making plans.

Arbron had become a general. He was just what the Living Hive needed. He could explain what the Taxxons would find when they erupted into the spaceport. He could explain how to hurt the Yeerks.

I don't know if he told the Hive how hopeless the task was. I only know that he seemed very alive. Almost on fire.

At last, he came to me. <Elfangor. There is a delicate problem we have to discuss. Alloran and the humans. You know what this will be like. Taxxon against Taxxon-Controller. Taxxon against Hork-Bajir. No one will be safe. From either side.>

<What do you want me to do?>

<If you can, find Alloran and the humans. I know that's what you'd want to do, anyway. But most importantly, get the Time Matrix safely away.

The Living Hive is no more safe from the Time Matrix than any other living thing.>

<I'll take care of the Time Matrix,> I said.

<You'll need to take the *Jahar*. I'll help get you to it.>

<And then you can leave with me,> I said.

<No, Elfangor. I'm staying here. We'll lose this battle. But there may be other chances to hurt the Yeerks.>

I didn't know what to say. I guess I felt like only Arbron could decide for Arbron now. <I'll . . . I'll tell your parents what —>

<No!> he said sharply. <No, Elfangor. Tell them I died in battle. Let them remember me the way I used to be, okay? I don't want them to remember me like this. I don't want them picturing me this way.>

<Arbron . . .> I said, my mind swimming in emotion.

<I have some last-minute planning. We've put that yellow machine of yours in one of the tubes. You'll go last, after all our people have been sent. Drive straight down the tunnel. The tunnel is part of the Hive. It will make sure you get to the right place. And one last thing . . .>

<Yes?>

<The spaceport will be hell,> he said flatly. <You won't be able to tell the difference between my

Taxxons and Taxxon-Controllers. So don't hesitate. Do what you have to.>

And then he left. The legs I had cut off were half grown back. But I could still recognize him, moving amongst the other Taxxons.

The launch of the attack was eerie to watch. Taxxons lined up alongside the tunnels. The Living Hive glowed a brighter red, and swiftly, smoothly, the Taxxons shoved through the slits in the tunnels and were blown down the tubes.

They were launched at a rate of one every eight seconds or so, down five separate tubes. It took almost half an hour for all the Taxxons to enter the tubes. And then it was my turn.

I nosed the yellow Mustang into the living, pulsating gap in the tube. To my amazement, the tube stretched for me and the machine. It flattened down and widened out, leaving just inches of clearance.

I felt the WHOOOOOSH! of air pressure. It blew me down the tube. I gunned the engine and went from zero to two hundred miles per hour in seconds!

There was nothing exhilarating about this. I was blasting down a living tunnel, enclosed on all sides, ducking my head to avoid having my stalk eyes scraped off. The only light came from the machine's own lights — white, looking ahead, red, looking back.

For long minutes I raced along beneath the surface of the Taxxon world. On my way to a massacre.

And then . . .

FWOOOOOSH!

I shot into the air.

RrrrrrEEEEEEEEEEEE! The engine screamed as the wheels spun madly in midair.

I burst from the ground, flew through the air, and saw, in flashes of explosion and Dracon-beam blast, a scene no madman could have dreamed.

The machine arced toward the ground.

WHHUUUUMPPPFF!

The front wheels hit, the engine roared, I was banged so badly that my elbow and left foreleg were scraped bloody, and the Mustang dug in and hauled away in an explosion of kicked-up dirt.

Suddenly, a Taxxon right in front of me!

SPLOOOMMMP!

The machine slammed into the Taxxon and burst it open like a bag of garbage!

<Aaaahhhh!> I screamed in sheer horror.

But it was only one small piece of horror in a scene that will be burned on my brain forever.

Taxxon cries!

Hork-Bajir roars!

The TSEEEWW TSEEEWW! of Dracon beams!

Scenes of nauseating violence were everywhere! The battle had already raged for half an hour. Half an hour of unarmed Taxxons against bladed Hork-Bajir.

It was a slaughterhouse.

How was I supposed to find the humans amidst that awful battle? How was I even supposed to think?

A huge Hork-Bajir spotted me and began to run for the Mustang. Only when he got close did he cry "Andalite!" in surprise and greedy delight.

He leaped at the moving machine. I spun the steering wheel. The Mustang turned sharply. I gunned the engine! WHUUMPF! I hit the Hork-Bajir in the legs. He cartwheeled over my head and landed in the dirt behind me.

Taxxons! Hork-Bajir! Gedds! All around me! I used the Mustang like a battering ram, mowing down anyone in my way.

The *Jahar*. All I could do was head for the *Jahar*!

The lovely ship stood proud above the slaughter. And there, atop the ship's cradle, clearly silhouetted by the lights, were two strange, alien shapes. Two aliens that walked on two legs alone, without tail.

The humans!

Seething around the base of the ship's cradle were a hundred Taxxons. All pushing and shoving to squeeze up the narrow ramp that led to the ship itself.

Standing alone on the ramp was a single Taxxon. A single Taxxon with four legs shorter than the rest.

<Arbron!> I screamed, as I slammed the Mustang into the mass of ravening Taxxons.

<Elfangor! I can't hold them any longer!>

<Are these Taxxon-Controllers? Or are they your soldiers?>

<There's no difference anymore, Elfangor! Don't you see? Blood has been spilled. The hunger . . . the hunger! Stop me, Elfangor! Stop me!>

And with that, Arbron, *aristh* of the Dome ship *StarSword*, lost his last shred of control. He turned from facing down the Taxxon mob. He turned and ran for the humans, mouth gaping open.

chapter 8

<Noooooo!> I screamed. I leapt from the machine and plowed into the mass of Taxxon bodies.

My tail whipped the air!

Strike! And push through.

Strike! And push through.

Strike! Strike! Strikestrikestrike!

I reached the ramp and leaped clear over the last Taxxon in my way. <Loren! Run! Arbron! Nooooo!>

I raced up the ramp. Arbron was closing in on the humans.

The human Chapman was free. And it was toward him that Arbron ran. The human Chapman screamed.

Arbron reared back, ready to slam his upper body down on the frail human.

<*Aristh* Arbron!> I cried. <*Aristh* Arbron, you will stop! You will do your duty!>

I don't know what made me say that. I don't know. I only know that Arbron hesitated. As Chapman cowered, helpless, Arbron remained poised.

Behind me, I saw the Taxxons falling back. And over them climbed and leaped a handful of Hork-Bajir warriors.

Seven feet tall. Blades on their wrists and elbows and knees. Blade horns raked forward from their sleek snake heads. Short, spiked tails twitching. Ripping bird feet clawing at Taxxon flesh to advance.

I realized I knew one of the Hork-Bajir. It was Sub-Visser Seven.

"Ah, so we meet again, Andalite!" he said, sounding delighted. "Elfangor, right? That was the name you yelled so defiantly at me as you escaped. I was so afraid the Taxxons might have gotten to you by now. And I so wanted you all for myself!"

For a moment no one moved. The injured Taxxons withdrew down the ramp to make way for the Hork-Bajir.

I was alone against half a dozen Hork-Bajir. Behind me, Arbron, who still eyed Loren hungrily. And with them, Chapman. Whose side was Chapman on now? And whose side was Arbron on?

"Surrender, Elfangor," Sub-Visser Seven practically purred. "I won't kill you. I'll just . . . use you. I'll leave this crude body and live inside your head. I'll wrap myself around your smug, arrogant Andalite brain and make you my slave. And with your Andalite morphing power, I'll run the galaxy before

I'm done! It's either that or death, Andalite. There's no third choice."

I saw Arbron turn away from Loren. He came to stand beside me, a massive, ten-foot-long worm. <Guess we're a long way from the good old *Star-Sword*, eh, Elfangor?> he said, with a touch of his old humor. <We are one lost, lonely pair of *arisths*. Tell the Yeerk scum to dream on, Elfangor. Tell him we are Andalites. We don't surrender.>

<You heard my friend, Sub-Visser Seven,> I said. <You want me? Come get me.>

In the great stories and legends, that kind of speech always scares the bad guys. In real life it doesn't work that way.

"Okay," Sub-Visser Seven said. "I will come get you. Cut him down! Cut him down!" he screamed in sudden rage.

His Hork-Bajir leaped for me. But the ramp was narrow. There was only room for two Hork-Bajir at a time. Any trained Andalite can handle a Hork-Bajir one-on-one. They're fast. We're faster.

SWOOOOOOSH! The first Hork-Bajir swung his wrist blade.

FWAAAPPPP! I struck with my tail, and he no longer had a wrist blade. Or a wrist.

But the second Hork-Bajir shoved past him and got to my left. One of his comrades swung over the railing and leaped onto the platform to our right. And the wounded Hork-Bajir was still dangerous.

The odds were getting worse very quickly. More Hork-Bajir were cramming onto the ramp, anxious to serve their sub-visser.

Battle exploded suddenly in rapid thrusts and slashes. Hork-Bajir blades made the air sing as they whipped their powerful arms and legs at me. Arbron did what he could, but a Taxxon is helpless in a blade fight. The Hork-Bajir just climbed over him to reach me.

"Elfangor! Look out!" Loren screamed.

"Get him! What are you waiting for?" Sub-Visser Seven roared. "He's just one Andalite!"

I fell back under the pressure. I had no time to think. None. Only time to react. Only time to block deadly blows. I had been cut badly already, and it was only a matter of time.

And then a new Hork-Bajir stepped forward. <So, how are you enjoying the war, *Aristh* Elfangor?> he asked in Andalite thought-speak.

I was so stunned I almost missed the next blow. War-prince Alloran! In Hork-Bajir morph!

Alloran spun. Before the sub-visser could so much as twitch, Alloran had pressed his wrist blade against the Yeerk's throat.

<Don't move, Yeerk. Don't even breathe,> Allo-

ran said. <Call off your men. Do it, or I'll laugh when your head goes rolling across the ground.>

"Hold!" the sub-visser cried. "Back away!"

The Hork-Bajir obeyed. They backed away. I panted and gasped for air. I was exhausted. I was bleeding. Loren ran over and pressed her hands against a deep gash in my chest. The pressure slowed the loss of blood.

"You're still alive!" she said. "I was so worried."

<Now here's what we're going to do,> Alloran said. <The two humans and my two friends and I are going aboard the *Jahar*. And you, Sub-Visser, are coming with us. Once we're off the cradle, we'll toss you back out. How does that plan sound to you, Yeerk?> he demanded, tightening his hold on the sub-visser.

"Do I have a choice?"

<There's always a choice, Yeerk. I can cut you right out of that Hork-Bajir and feed your impotent slug body to my friend the Taxxon here. That's one choice. Or you can order your men back down the ramp. All the way down.>

"Whatever became of the Andalite reputation for kindness and gentleness?" the Yeerk mocked.

<What happened? We left that image in the ashes of the Hork-Bajir home world.>

"You were there?"

<I was there. My name is Alloran-Semitur-Corrass. War-prince Alloran.>

For the first time, the sub-visser seemed afraid. His mocking, arrogant attitude seemed to evaporate. He quickly ordered his Hork-Bajir down the ramp.

Together we backed carefully toward the *Jahar*. Alloran, with the Yeerk sub-visser in his steel grip; Loren, still tending my wound; and Chapman, the treacherous human who had led us all to this terrible mess.

Only Arbron turned away from the open hatch of the *Jahar*.

<Come with us, Arbron,> I said. <Look around. The free Taxxons have lost. The Living Hive will be destroyed. There's no future for you here.>

<Elfangor, there's no future for me anywhere.>

<But you can't,> I said. <Who's going to remind me not to be so stiff? Who's going to laugh at me when I start talking about being a great prince?>

<You go, Elfangor,> Arbron said gently. <Go save the galaxy.>

<Leave him,> Alloran said. <*Aristh* . . . I mean, *Warrior* Arbron is a casualty of war.>

chapter 9

We launched the <u>Jahar</u>. There was no one to stop us. The battle still raged, and none of the Yeerks had the presence of mind to come after us.

Or so I thought.

Alloran demorphed from his Hork-Bajir body. I was relieved. I guess he saw my expression.

<Did you think I had ended up like Arbron back there? Trapped? A *nothlit*? No, *Aristh* Elfangor. I am still myself.>

<I'm glad, sir,> I said.

Sub-Visser Seven stood in a corner, eyeing Alloran as he demorphed and resumed his usual Andalite body. Loren seemed dazed. Even Chapman seemed unusually quiet. No doubt he was afraid of what we would do to him.

He deserved *whatever* we did to him.

<Your orders, sir?> I asked the prince.

Alloran sneered. <Ah. Now you want orders. When I ordered you to flush those pools full of Yeerks out into space you disobeyed me. But now

you want orders. Now you *want* to be told what to do.>

I was too tired to be angry. I was even too tired to consider how my earlier refusal to follow orders would probably destroy my career. What was I going to do? Explain to some military tribunal that I, the insignificant *aristh*, had thought Alloran's order immoral?

<Sir, the Time Matrix is —>

<Silence, you young fool!> Alloran snapped angrily. He glared at me, enraged. <We don't have time for that yet. No, first we have to take care of the business you kept me from taking care of. That Taxxon ship full of Yeerks is still in its cradle. Still filled with Yeerk slugs. What do you think I've been doing the last day and a half? I've been hiding in shadows, morphing and demorphing, watching that ship.>

<Prince Alloran, is that really the most important thing to do?>

For the first time since he had demorphed, he turned to face me. He glared at me with his main eyes. And that's when I saw the look. That's when I saw the rage. The mad rage.

<The most important thing in war is to destroy your enemies, *Aristh* Elfangor. Nothing is more important than destroying your enemies. Do you understand?>

He turned his stalk eyes toward the sub-visser. <You understand, don't you? You Yeerks understand.>

"You said you would let me go!" the sub-visser cried.

<And so I will,> Alloran said. <Open the hatch, *Aristh* Elfangor. The sub-visser is going to see if that Hork-Bajir body of his can fly!>

The sub-visser tensed up. He was not going to get pushed out of a spaceship without a fight. His Hork-Bajir muscles bunched and rippled.

He seemed to glance at Chapman. And I swear . . . but, no, I had to be imagining things. It's just that Chapman seemed to shake his head, almost invisibly.

The sub-visser's face glazed over. His eyes went dead. He relaxed his muscles.

<Slow to dead stop,> Alloran ordered. <Altitude?>

<Fifteen thousand feet,> I said dully. <We are still within the atmosphere. Air speed is now at dead stop.>

<Dead stop,> Alloran said. <Appropriate. Now open the hatch.>

What could I do? I was just an *aristh*. I had already defied Alloran once. If I defied him again. . . . He was mad. Insane.

What could I do?

I opened the hatch. Warm Taxxon air blew in, strange in the enclosed environment. It ruffled Loren's golden hair.

<Get out, Yeerk,> Alloran said to Sub-Visser Seven.

I closed my main eyes. I kept my stalk eyes focused on my instruments. I could not look.

<Close the hatch,> Alloran said a few seconds later.

I dared to look. The sub-visser was gone. I looked down at the exterior display screens. A tiny figure fell through the clouds. I looked away.

<Now we go back and fry that transport ship,> Alloran said briskly. <Good to see you've grown up a little, *Aristh* Elfangor. Take us back over the southeastern corner of the spaceport. Maintain present altitude. Then we'll go pick up our missing Time Matrix, eh?>

He seemed cheerful. As if, for a moment at least, the madness were past. But I knew it wasn't over. We didn't need to destroy the Yeerks in those transport pools. We needed to secure the Time Matrix.

But I had given up arguing. I was tired. I was scared. I was sick from thinking of Arbron. I wanted to sleep and sleep and sleep, and not wake up till I was home on my own grass, under my own trees.

I saw Loren watching me. She seemed worried. Concerned. Who wouldn't be? And yet . . .

Chapman was watching, too. He seemed tense. Understandable. And yet . . .

<What made you decide to come with us?> I asked Chapman. <Do you expect mercy from us? You betrayed us. You betrayed your fellow human. You've told the Yeerks about Earth. You may have betrayed your entire species.>

He shrugged. "Not my fault, though, is it? I was on Earth, minding my own business. I didn't ask to be kidnapped by the Skrit Na. I didn't ask to be dragged halfway across the galaxy by you Andalites. I was just trying to protect myself."

<By making deals with the Yeerks?> Alloran laughed. <The Yeerks don't make deals. They enslave.>

"Yeah, I guess that's what I realized. After a while," Chapman said. "Look, I'm sorry, okay? I'm just a dumb human kid, okay? Give me a break."

<We are coming back over the spaceport,> I announced. <There is a lot of smoke. But you should still be able to get a good targeting lock with the shredder.>

Alloran didn't answer. He just stared at the display screen. At full magnification we could see the wormlike Taxxons below. We could easily see the ships, some burning from the battle, some tilted wildly over.

The Living Hive had done damage to the Yeerks.

But we could also see platoons of Hork-Bajir rounding up Taxxons. And other Taxxons were busily feeding . . .

Somewhere down there was Arbron.

Alloran aimed the shredder. He aimed it carefully, taking his time. He focused it on the transport ship that contained thousands of helpless Yeerk slugs.

<Fire, *Aristh* Elfangor,> he said.

<What?>

<I said fire. Fry those Yeerks. You let them live, now you finish them. Undo your mistake, and no one will ever havc to know about your earlier cowardice.>

My finger reached for the firing pad.

<Do it, Elfangor,> Alloran hissed.

chapter 10

My finger hovered above the pad. It was war. In war, you destroyed your enemies. Alloran was my prince. You obeyed your prince.

But ten thousand defenseless Yeerks? With one movement of my finger?

No.

I pulled my hand away, and in a blur of motion I felt Alloran's tail blade press against my throat. <You think you can fight a clean war, Elfangor? Is that what you think? Or are you one of those who are happy enough when someone like me does the dirty work for you?>

<They are defenseless,> I said as calmly as I could.

<They are the enemy. Hypocrites! You're all hypocrites! We lost the Hork-Bajir war because of weak, moralizing fools like you! Because of fools like you, I am disgraced and shunned and sent off on trivial errands with nothing but *arisths* under my command.>

<War-prince Alloran, I honor you, but —>

<What is the difference how you destroy the enemy?> Alloran demanded.

I had no idea what he was talking about anymore. He was off somewhere in his own head. Lost in his own memories.

<What does it matter if you kill them with a tail blade or a shredder or a quantum virus?>

Quantum virus? No. No. Even after all the horror I had seen, I was shocked.

<You . . . you used a quantum virus? You used a quantum virus on the Hork-Bajir world?>

A quantum virus is a sort of disease of spacetime. You see, it slowly breaks down the force that holds subatomic particles together. It slowly disintegrates whatever it affects. Living creatures affected with a quantum virus find their very molecules breaking down. It can take days, weeks of agony.

That was Alloran's secret. That was his disgrace. The Yeerks had accused us of using a quantum virus against them. We had denied it. Every Andalite believed it was just another filthy Yeerk lie.

Alloran stared at me. <I cannot have a weak, cowardly fool like you messing up —>

I saw it out of the corner of my stalk eyes. A sudden movement. Not fast, but unexpected.

Chapman!

He leaped at Alloran and swung one of his strong human hands. With tightly clenched fingers he hit Alloran on the side of his head.

Alloran's head snapped back. More in surprise than pain. But it was enough. I swung my tail hard and fast. I turned the blade away and slammed Alloran's head with every ounce of power I had.

He dropped like a stone. He collapsed to the deck in a heap. And I saw triumph on Chapman's face. Triumph.

I should have known then. I should have realized.

Instead, I went to the medical kit and with shaking hands pulled out a tranquilizer hypo. I emptied it into my mad prince. It would keep him down for hours.

"Now what?" Chapman demanded.

<Now what?!> I shrieked. <Now what? I just knocked out my own prince!> I was sick. Sick down to my bones. But there was no one else to turn to. No one else to make decisions. As stupid as I had been, it was still up to me.

<We have something to pick up,> I said, forcing calm into my thought-speak voice. <Then we are getting as far from this evil place as this ship will go!>

Chapman nodded, as if satisfied.

Loren came over. She put her soft human hand

on my chest wound. It had begun to scab over but the exertion of knocking Alloran out had opened the wound again. She tore a strip of fabric from the bottom of one of her artificial skins. She tied it around my chest to protect the wound.

<Thank you,> I said.

"Is life always this insane for you space cadets?"

<Oh, yes,> I said bitterly. <Infiltrate the Taxxon home world, help inspire a Taxxon civil war, mutiny against my prince, and locate the Time Matrix, all in the company of a pair of strange, two-legged aliens. . . . Business as usual.>

I was busy watching the ground below, looking for the place where I had crashed the Skrit Na ship. But I saw Loren's smile.

"Hey. You made a joke. I didn't think you did humor, Elfangor."

<When the world goes mad, what else can you do?> I thought of Arbron. Still making little jokes, even when his life was a wreck. <I wonder if Arbron knew the world was mad?>

Loren just looked sad. But then she forced a smile again. "Speaking of crazy . . . did I see you driving up in a bright yellow Mustang back there?"

<It was a wonderful machine. Primitive, but strangely enjoyable.>

I cut thrust and peered closely into the screen. <There it is. We're going down. I need to clear away

the wreckage so the tractor beam can grab the Time Matrix.>

I landed the *Jahar* in the narrow valley, a few feet away from the wreckage of the Skrit Na ship. I grabbed a handheld shredder, opened the hatch, and hurried outside.

It took several minutes to burn away the wreckage of the Skrit Na ship and reveal the Time Matrix.

It was for this that so much horror had occurred.

For this most powerful of all weapons.

It sat there amidst the wreckage, so harmless-looking. If the Yeerks had known this was here, they would have stopped at nothing to get it.

It was lucky Loren never told them while they held her captive. Lucky that Chapman never told them.

Lucky.

And lucky that I had been able to hold off the Hork-Bajir. And lucky that we had been able to get away from the spaceport without being pursued.

More luck.

Too much luck.

I really was a fool. I felt a cold shiver crawl up my spine.

I was behind the Time Matrix, hidden from the *Jahar*. And suddenly, I knew what was happening back inside the *Jahar* while I worked to free the

Time Matrix. And I knew what I would see when I walked back around that off-white globe.

Trembling with despair and exhaustion, I set the shredder for its next to lowest setting. I would have to duplicate Arbron's feat: three quick shots. Yes. *Three.*

I sucked in deep breaths, and then I bolted at top speed.

I leaped from behind the Time Matrix.

Loren, raising a Dracon beam in her hand!

I fired!

She dropped, twitching wildly from the energy pulse.

TSSSEEEWWWW!

Chapman fired! But he was weak and shaky from what he had just endured.

I fired! The human dropped to the dirt.

But there was one more left. I knew it. I knew, and I knew that I had very little time.

Sudden movement! I spun and fired! Missed! No, not a complete miss. I had stunned his right arm. The hand holding the Dracon beam dropped, useless.

He stood there, rage on his face. Alloran. War-prince Alloran-Semitur-Corrass.

But not really Alloran anymore.

For the rest of my life I would remember that

moment. The moment when I looked for the first time, upon the abomination.

You see, Alloran was no longer Alloran.

<Very good, *Aristh* Elfangor. It took you a while, but you figured it out in the end.>

<Sub-Visser Seven,> I said.

<Yes, but not for long. The Yeerk who made the first Andalite-Controller? The Yeerk who captured the fabled Time Matrix? I'd say I can count on a major promotion. Wouldn't you?>

chapter 11

I raised my shredder and pointed it at Alloran . . . no, at Sub-Visser Seven.

<You made Chapman a Controller. You were in his head. That Hork-Bajir I thought was you . . . just a trick.>

<Of course. And another of my people made Loren one of us,> he sneered. <And while you so considerately worked to clear away the Time Matrix, I revived Alloran and transferred myself into him. The first and only Andalite-Controller! It was so kind of you to knock the old warrior out for me. I didn't know how I was ever going to take him. He was a wily creature. A bit mad, of course, but he knew war. You saw how ruthless he was in tossing out the poor Hork-Bajir who played the role of me. Yes, Alloran was a warrior.>

The truth hit me like a brick wall. It was true! I had made it possible for the sub-visser to take control of Alloran!

I had created the abomination!

<Chapman told us about the Time Matrix, of

course. But we needed you to show us where it was. The attack by the Mountain Taxxons could have disrupted everything, but you know, in the end it was convenient. It kept you from growing suspicious. You were too busy worrying about your fellow *aristh*. You didn't even have time to wonder how the two humans just happened to be waiting for you. You didn't wonder why my troops let you escape.>

I had done this! I had created this abomination! I had delivered the Time Matrix into the hands of this vile creature!

<But you know the best part?> The sub-visser laughed. <I really couldn't have let you burn that transport ship full of my people. Chapman didn't know about the Yeerks in that transport, so neither did I. And if you'd gone along with Alloran I'd have had to try to stop you. So would my brother Yeerk in the human girl. It was one thing to sacrifice the poor fool who played the role of me. But ten thousand Yeerks? No, I'd have had to act, and then you and Alloran together would have most likely made short work of me.>

I couldn't breathe. I had failed. Failed so enormously that the entire Andalite species was at risk!

<But no, Elfangor is one of those good Andalites,> Sub-Visser Seven sneered. <You don't go in for slaughtering the helpless, do you? Hah-hah!

Wonderful! Your qualms delivered Alloran to me. Alloran and the Time Matrix. Mine!>

<Really?> I said faintly. <I seem to be the one holding the shredder.>

<There are a dozen Bug fighters closing in right now. You've lost, little one.>

<You'll be a cinder by the time they get here,> I threatened.

<No, you won't kill a helpless foe,> he sneered. <I have no weapon! I am your prisoner! Hah-hah! I surrender to you, Elfangor. I surrender!>

He spread his hands in a gesture of helplessness as he laughed at me. Laughed.

<You're right, Sub-Visser. I won't kill you.> I squeezed the trigger. The stun-setting knocked the foul Andalite-Controller to the ground.

I ran to Loren. I dragged her unconscious body up the ramp into the *Jahar*. Then, after a second's hesitation, I dragged Chapman aboard, too.

I was just beginning to try dragging the sub-visser to the ship when the first wave of Bug fighters blew by overhead. They shot past, then began to inscribe tight circles, coming back toward us.

Two more Bug fighters. Then two more. The sky was filling with Bug fighters. I would never get the *Jahar* off the planet.

Unless . . .

Had Sub-Visser Seven informed his people that

he might be in an Andalite body? Surely. Surely he would have. He would have had to, just to avoid being accidentally shot by his own people.

But could the Yeerks tell one Andalite from another?

I raced to the ship, tore open the medical kit and yanked out a stimulant hypo. I ran back to the unconscious sub-visser and I emptied the stimulant into his bloodstream. It would revive him in less than a minute.

Bug fighters were hovering overhead now, some preparing to land. I ran back to the *Jahar*, closed the hatch, and punched up the ship-to-ship communication.

The face of a Hork-Bajir-Controller appeared on my communications screen. It stared at me with the fury and distaste Yeerks always show for Andalites.

I stared straight back. And in loud, arrogant, harsh thought-speak I said, <What? You don't recognize your sub-visser? Hah-hah! I have done it, you fool! As I said I would. I have acquired an Andalite body!>

The Hork-Bajir eyes wavered, uncertain.

If I showed any hesitation, I was lost. If I was to pass as a Yeerk sub-visser, I could not show any doubt. <You see the Andalite down on the ground?>

"Yes . . . Sub-Visser Seven."

<Good, you're not blind as well as stupid. I want to see him run. Do you understand me! As soon as I have lifted off, make him run! And then, when he is good and tired, when his knees buckle with exhaustion, make him dead. Dead! And if you fail me, I will feed you to the Taxxons. Sub-Visser Seven, out.>

I switched off the screen without waiting for an answer. Maybe it would work. Maybe not.

I keyed the controls, lifting the *Jahar* gently from the ground. I switched on an exterior view and panned the viewfinder till I framed the sub-visser. He was just climbing to his feet.

I'll give the sub-visser credit for one thing: He was not an idiot. He knew instantly what was happening. He broke into a run, just as a hovering Bug fighter fired a Dracon beam near him.

I let the *Jahar* drift casually over the Skrit Na wreck. Focusing all my attention, I powered the *Jahar*'s tractor beam and latched it onto the white sphere of the Time Matrix.

Sub-Visser Seven was running at full Andalite speed across the sand, pursued by teasing, taunting Bug fighters that seemed to enjoy shooting within inches of him.

The *Jahar* rose, with the Time Matrix in tow. I pulled the machine closer and closer, snugged it up into the *Jahar*'s belly, and lashed it in place with energy ropes. We rose up through the atmosphere of the Taxxon world. Up through the weird, bright clouds.

Only then did it begin to dawn on the Yeerks.

The ship-to-ship snapped on. An ugly, suspicious Hork-Bajir face glared at me. "Sub-Visser Seven, planet control respectfully directs you to land."

I tried bluffing some more. But when I refused to immediately turn back and land, they knew.

Tactical showed a swarm of Bug fighters rising up from the surface of the planet. But it was too late.

I punched up a hard burn and prepared to lose myself in Zero-space.

chapter 12

"So, this is Zero-space," Loren said, looking out through the viewport. "We've been in it for a full day and I still don't understand what it is."

I directed my stalk eyes to the viewport. I saw blank white. Empty, whiteness. <Zero-space isn't anything, really,> I said quietly. <It's antispace. You know, like antimatter and antigravity? Well, Zero-space Is antispace.>

I had explained this at least twice during the last day. But I guess she was trying to make conversation.

She'd been through one of the worst experiences any creature can endure: She had been made a Controller. I couldn't believe she was even managing to talk without weeping.

Fortunately, the Yeerk in Loren's head had been at the end of its feeding cycle. Yeerks feed on Kandrona rays. Every three days they must drain out of their host and return to the Yeerk pool to absorb Kandrona rays.

So I made a deal with the hungry Yeerk. I could

keep Loren tied up and wait for the Yeerk to starve to death. Or the Yeerk could come out willingly. I agreed to put it in deep hibernation. To freeze it. The Yeerk decided hibernation was better than death by Kandrona ray starvation.

I kept my word to the Yeerk. After it crawled out of Loren's ear, I froze it. And then I ejected it from the ship into the vacuum of real space. Someday it might be found and revived. More likely it would sink into the gravity well of a star and be incinerated.

Especially since I made sure to eject it close to a sun.

Maybe that wasn't living up to the spirit of my deal with the Yeerk. But somehow, I just didn't care. My notions of proper behavior had brought disaster.

I was a fool. A silly child living out storybook notions of decency and fairness.

There was no decency in war. Alloran had tried to teach me that. I'd learned it too late.

"Have you decided where we're going, Elfangor?" Loren asked gently.

"He doesn't know," Chapman said. He spent his time now sitting in a corner, glaring darkly at the two of us. Sub-Visser Seven had been inside Chapman's head. If that had taught the foolish human a lesson, it sure didn't show. "Elfangor is confused. Isn't that right? He screwed up bad . . . Arbron trapped in one of those centipede bodies, Alloran made into the first-ever Andalite-Controller. Almost lost the Time Matrix. Gonna be tough explaining all this to the folks back home, eh?"

I ignored him. Back home. What was home anymore? Was I supposed to return home? Home to my parents? Run free on my old, familiar grass? Spend my days with my old childhood friends?

I wasn't a child anymore. My home was still there, but I would never belong there again.

Loren came over to me. "Elfangor. Snap out of it. We're going in circles in Zero-space."

<Yes. I know.>

"You did the best you could. You're just a kid, like me."

<I am an *aristh* in the Andalite military. I disobeyed my prince and caused him to be enslaved by the Yeerks. The Yeerks will now learn everything Alloran knows about our defenses. Everything he knows about the capabilities of our weapons. Everything he knows about the locations of our ships. At least he wasn't a scientist, so he can't give them morphing technology or computer software. But he will still be the greatest intelligence victory in Yeerk history.>

Chapman shook his head. "Guess I was right to throw in with the Yeerks, eh? You Andalites are going down. Unless . . ."

Loren glared at him. "Why don't you shut up?"

Chapman just grinned. "Unless you Andalites use the Time Matrix thing. Go back in time, find that first little tribe of Yeerk slugs. Kill 'em and the entire Yeerk species is gone. Gone and never even existed. What do they call that? Oh yeah, genocide. You up for a little genocide, Elfangor?"

I just shook my head wearily. <Don't waste your time taunting me, Chapman. It won't work.>

Loren looked puzzled. "What do you mean?"

<He's trying to goad me into using the Time Matrix. Remember, he's been a Controller, however briefly. Sub-Visser Seven left him instructions, just in case something went wrong. Chapman knows that to use the Time Matrix I'd have to return to real space. My guess is that the Yeerks placed a homing beacon on the *Jahar*. If we return to normal space, we'll light up every Yeerk sensor within a million light years.>

I could see from the dark rage on Chapman's face that I had guessed correctly.

At least I'd gotten one thing right. I wasn't fool enough to fall for —

Suddenly, it was as if a light had gone on in my head. Wherever the *Jahar* emerged into real space, the Yeerks would go tearing after it.

No matter where.

A trap! I could spring a trap!

But where? Where should I draw the Yeerk fleet?

To the *StarSword*! My old ship. She was off pursuing a Yeerk task force near the Graysha Nebula. She'd been hoping to meet a second Dome ship there.

Two Dome ships. Plus the *Jahar*. Enough firepower to handle just about anything the Yeerks could muster.

I went to the control panel and entered the coordinates.

"You have a plan?" Loren asked.

<More or less,> I muttered. I was already having doubts. <There's a place called the Graysha Nebula. We don't know much about it. But there are rumors of a sentient species living in that area. And there are rumors that the Yeerks are exploring the nebula. My old ship, the *StarSword*, went there to see if it could locate a Yeerk task force we were pursuing.>

"So we're going there to meet up with your old ship. Is . . . is this nebula place closer to Earth?"

<No.>

"Elfangor . . . am I ever going to get back home?"

<Loren, I will do my best.>

Chapman snorted. "And you've seen how good Elfangor's best is. You might as well kiss Earth goodbye."

chapter 13

<We will emerge into real space,> I explained. <If we're lucky, we won't be far from the *StarSword*. If we're even luckier, there will be additional Andalite ships close by. From that point it will only take the Yeerks an hour or so to start showing up.>

"And then?" Loren asked.

<Space battle, I suppose. Andalite fighters and Yeerk Bug fighters going at it. Us, too, of course.>

"Is there anything I can do to help?"

<Yes. Show me the best way to tie up a human,> I said, looking at Chapman. <I don't want any distractions.>

We tied the human around his feet and hands using spare conduit hose. Then we tied the hands to the feet behind his back.

"One last thing," Loren said. She took a short length of the hose and wrapped it around Chapman's face, covering his mouth. "Now we won't have to listen to him."

It took me a few seconds to understand. Many

species communicate by making sounds with their mouths. But it had never occurred to me you could silence someone with a piece of hose.

<To silence an Andalite you'd have to knock him out,> I said. <This won't hurt him?>

"No. Unfortunately." She smiled to show she had been joking.

After all she had been through, from being kidnapped by Skrit Na to being made a Controller, she could still laugh. I wondered if I'd been wrong to think humor was a weakness. I wondered if Arbron could still laugh.

"Elfangor . . . aren't you tempted by what Chapman said? I mean, if it were me, I might want to use that Time machine thing to change things. You know?"

<Like maybe go back in time and avoid getting kidnapped by the Skrit Na to begin with?>

She laughed. "No. Not that. Look, my life was pretty dull before all this. I know when you take me back to Earth you'll have to erase all my memories of this. But still, even though it was horrible sometimes, I don't think I'd want to never have met you. If it wasn't for my mom worrying and all . . ."

I was surprised. And pleased, too. <In the Skrit Na ship, where I found the Mustang, I also found pictures of Earth. It looked very beautiful. Wonderful, delicious-looking grass and tall trees and

streams of water that bubbled across stones. Is your home like that?>

"We do have places like that," Loren said, smiling sadly. "There's a place we went once, back when I was little and my dad was still with us. Before he went to the war. It's a place called Yosemite. We camped out in a tent. Yosemite is like that."

<And did you stick small white cylinders in your mouth and smile at the beauty of it all?>

"Small white cylinders?" Loren looked puzzled. Then she laughed her strange but delightful human laugh. "You were looking at cigarette ads! Those white cylinders are called cigarettes. They're bad for you, actually. Very bad for you. They make you sick."

<So . . . so humans go to beautiful places and use sickening cylinders? Why?>

But Loren was laughing too hard to answer. And pretty soon, even though I had no idea what was so funny, I was laughing, too. Although my laugh could only be heard by Loren inside her own head.

"So," she said after a while. "Why don't *you* want to use this Time Matrix thing?"

I waved my stalks forward and back in a gesture of uncertainty. <You can't just go messing around with time. They say it's insanely complicated. Sure, maybe I could go back, like Chapman said, and stomp out the first Yeerks who evolved. But who

knows how many other things that might affect? Besides, to be honest, I guess I'm scared of the Ellimists.>

"The what?"

<Supposedly they're the race that built the Time Matrix. Thousands and thousands of years ago. They built it, and then, suddenly, as far as anyone can tell, they vanished. The entire species of Ellimists just vanished.>

"You think it was because they used the Time Matrix?"

<No one knows. Some people say the Ellimists still exist, but they've moved beyond the normal space-time dimensions we know. There are some who say the Ellimists are almost all-powerful.> I shrugged. <Of course, there are others who say they're gone forever. Or even that they never did exist. Now Andalite parents tell their children stories about the Ellimists.>

"Fairy tales."

<Are fairies magical beings in human mythology?>

"Not just fairies. We have elves and leprechauns and Santa Claus and hobbits and werewolves and vampires. . . . We even have aliens from outer space."

Despite myself, I laughed. <Yes, those outer space aliens are quite troublesome.>

"Doesn't the Time Matrix prove that these Ellimists are real?"

<Well . . . I don't know. But if Ellimists *are* real, if they really do live in dimensions beyond our own, then they have powers we could not imagine. Pretend . . . never mind.>

"No, tell me," Loren urged. "Unless you have something else to do."

<Okay, well, you know that space-time has ten dimensions. There are the normal dimensions of up/down, left/right, and forward/back. Then there is the fourth dimension, which is time. Then, there are six other dimensions, but they are curled up into themselves, so we don't see or feel them. All we feel are three space dimensions, plus time.>

Loren nodded her head. I wondered what this meant. But she didn't ask me to stop, so I went on.

<Imagine if, instead of three normal space dimensions, we only had two. Imagine we were flat, and we couldn't go up or down, just in the other two directions. Call us the Flatties. See?>

"Like if we lived on a piece of paper," Loren said.

<Exactly. It would be like we were drawings on a piece of paper. And if someone came along and drew a box around us, we could never get out. Because the lines of the box would be walls. But what if a three-dimensional person came along? A three-dimensional person could lift that Flattie right up

out of that box. The Flattie wouldn't even know what was happening, because he's never gone up or down before. He doesn't even know up and down exist.>

"You're saying we're like the Flatties. Except we're in three dimensions, not just two. So we're like Cubies or something."

<Yes. So if some creature came along who existed in more dimensions than us, he'd be able to do things that would be impossible for us.>

"Ellimists. That's what they are?"

<Maybe. Like I say, no one knows. But someone built the Time Matrix. Someone real. Someone who isn't around anymore.>

"Whew."

<So maybe we could use the Time Matrix and pop in and out of time. Or maybe we'd disappear, like the Ellimists may have.>

"Or maybe we'd just make these Ellimists mad," Loren said.

<Exactly.>

"But if you give the Time Matrix to your people, won't they use it, anyway? Even with all the risks?"

<A week ago I'd have said absolutely not. I'd have said we Andalites don't do things like that. Not even in war.>

"But now . . . whatever Alloran did on that Hork-Bajir planet, it was wrong, wasn't it?"

I stared at her with my main eyes. <Loren, I don't know what's right or wrong anymore. I just don't.>

The computer signaled that we were nearing the translation point.

<We're going back to normal space,> I said. <And by the way . . . if we do survive all this, and get you back to Earth, could you show me this place with the grass and trees and tall waterfalls?>

"It's a date," Loren said.

<Could we have a Mustang there, too?>

She put her arm around my waist and looked deep into my eyes with her two tiny blue human eyes. "Anything you want, Elfangor. Just no white cylinders."

chapter 14

<Coming out of Zero-space . . . now!>

Zero-space is dead white. Normal space is usually deep black, dotted with stars that burn in bright white and pale red and cold blue.

But this space was not like that.

"Jeez! Amazing!"

<You've never been close to a nebula,> I observed. But the truth was, even I was awed.

The nebula was a dust cloud so large that a dozen solar systems the size of Earth's could have been lost in it with room to spare. It was like a weird, twisted cloud. A cloud of purple and orange that seemed to envelop brilliant stars.

"It's so beautiful!"

<Yes. And if the *StarSword* is out there somewhere, it'll really be beautiful.>

I glanced over at Chapman. He lay trussed up and gagged. He glared back at me.

<Right now Yeerk ships are hearing the transponder they attached to us. They'll be on us in a very short time. I'm conducting a sensor sweep,

looking for any Andalite vessels. But it's hard with the nebula around us. The dust confuses the sensors.>

"Are we a long way from Earth?"

<Yes. Even by the standards of space. We are hundreds of light-years away.>

Loren stared out at the nebula. She bit her lip a little with her teeth and took her arm away from my waist.

Humans like to use touch. It seems odd at first. But I had gotten used to it.

<I'm going to try calling the *StarSword*,> I said.

I made the thought-speak link with the communications system. <Any Andalite ship this sector, any Andalite ship this sector. This is *Jahar*.>

I expected to have to wait. I was shocked when I heard the voice of Captain Feyorn. <*Jahar! Jahar!* Alloran, is that you? We are under attack. Say again, under attack. Can you —>

<*StarSword*, I lost you! *StarSword!*> I checked the display. Yes, we had a location fix! I punched in the new heading.

<Loren, get down on the ground. Back against the bulkhead. I'm going to Maximum Burn!>

She ran and threw herself down on the ground, just as I punched in the burn. But the acceleration was barely noticeable. The *Jahar* had amazingly good compensators. But even though there was no feeling of acceleration, the ship blew through space.

"Elfangor, what's going on?"

<I don't know. But I'm powering up all weapons.>

At Maximum Burn it took less than ten minutes for us to be able to spot the great Dome ship. She came up on my view screen at high magnification. She looked like a glowing steel stick with a bright half-ball on one end. Her engines were off. In the space around her were a dozen or more of our fighters.

But what caught my attention were the asteroids — rough, dark tumbling rocks. The *StarSword* seemed to be in the middle of an asteroid field. Only that was unlikely. Asteroids orbited stars. There was no star close enough to hold an asteroid field in its gravity.

"Hey! It moved!" Loren said.

<What are you talking about?> I demanded. I sounded rude because I was busy trying to figure out what was going on. And I didn't think a human was going to be very helpful, really.

"Those rocks. Those asteroids. Look! Look at them!"

I turned one stalk eye to watch the asteroids. Then, in a flash, I focused all four eyes.

<They're moving! They are under power!>

As we stared, transfixed, one of the asteroids seemed to sprout a tail. It was a plume of hot plasma! The asteroid turned! It changed course, and shot toward one of the *StarSword*'s fighters.

The fighter fired a full-power shredder blast at the asteroid. The green beam zapped through the vacuum. The asteroid glowed where the shredder blast hit, and then it increased speed.

The fighter turned to run. But to my amazement, the asteroid accelerated. It stayed on the fighter's tail, twisting, turning, accelerating and then . . .

"Oh! Elfangor, look!"

<No! It's impossible!>

A pillar of living rock extended from the asteroid like some primitive arm. It struck the fighter. I saw a tiny puff as the air was squeezed from the ship.

And then the rock simply grew over the doomed ship. It grew swift, unstoppable, until, within seconds, the entire fighter was covered by living rock.

The asteroid had eaten a fighter.

chapter 15

"What <u>are</u> those things?" Loren asked in horror.

<I don't know. I've never seen or heard of anything like them. I mean, they are impossible!>

"They're like living asteroids or something."

<I think that's exactly what they are. But that's impossible.>

As I watched in horror, a second fighter was caught and swallowed up by a living rock.

<The *StarSword* will start shooting now,> I said confidently. <A Dome ship's shredders can blow chunks off a planet. They'll wipe these things out!>

TSEEEEWWWWW! TSEEEEWWWWW!

I had never seen the *StarSword*'s main shredders fire before. It was awesome. The beams of green light looked as thick as tree trunks as they blasted through space and hit one of the asteroids with enough power to punch a hole through a moon.

The asteroid glowed brightly. But it did not explode. It did not disintegrate. It did not melt.

It *turned*!

<It's going after the *StarSword*!>

Dozens of the asteroids seemed to be swarming the space around the *StarSword*. Close by, not three hundred miles away, I saw another fighter, twisting and turning, trying to lose one of the rocks.

<Go to Zero-space!> I yelled. <Whatever these things are, they can't have Zero-space flight!>

I guess the fighter pilot thought the same thing. I saw his engines glow bright as he powered up for a Zero-space jump. Suddenly, three more asteroids closed in on the fighter. They blocked its path. A massive arm of rock shot out and punched right into the fighter.

The pilot was blown clear. Out into empty space. He kicked his hooves for a few seconds. Then he stopped moving.

"Oh, God!"

<No! No! Noooo!>

The *StarSword* fired all shredders, lighting up black space with brilliant beams of light. But it didn't work. In fact, it seemed to draw more asteroids.

"Hey! That's just attracting them," Loren cried. "The engines and the weapons — they attract them!"

<You're right!> I don't know which shocked me more. That these asteroids were drawn to energy discharges. Or that it was the human girl who had figured it out.

I punched up communications. <*StarSword*, *StarSword*, this is *Jahar*. The asteroids are attracted by energy discharge! You're drawing them to you!>

I don't know if my message got through or not. But just then, I realized we had a whole new set of problems. Behind us, two Yeerk ships materialized, entering real space! They were no more than five thousand miles away.

A Pool ship, like a fat, awkward, three-legged spider. As soon as it appeared in real space, it began launching Bug fighters.

And beside the Pool ship, something I had never seen before. It was jet black so that it was barely visible. It was smaller than the Pool ship, but bigger than a Bug fighter. What seemed to be the bridge was a hard-edged diamond attached by a long triangular shaft to twin engines. The engines were a strange shape, like the blades of a two-headed ax.

The entire thing looked like some ancient weapon — a battle ax. It was like some flying Hork-Bajir. A Blade ship.

Don't ask me how I knew. I don't believe in psychic things, although some Andalites do. But still, I knew who was in that Blade ship.

I felt cold hatred. Hatred of that black ship. Hatred of the abomination I had helped to create.

<So. He's still alive,> I whispered. <This time, no mercy.>

Space was filling up quickly. Yeerk ships, Andalite ships, and the deadly, impossible asteroids. But the Yeerks were thousands of miles behind me, and I was thousands of miles from the Andalite fleet. If I was lucky, the Yeerks would not be able to see the Dome ship on their sensors yet.

And they would not even be looking for murderous asteroids.

The computer blinked to show an incoming communication. It was visual as well as thought-speak. The image that appeared on the screen was Andalite.

The familiar face of Alloran-Semitur-Corrass. But from that familiar face shone an evil that I cannot describe.

<Ah, Elfangor, I believe,> Sub-Visser Seven said. <Still have the Time Matrix, I hope? I'm here to take it from you.>

I had not yet switched on my own image for him to see. I had to think fast. I grabbed a handheld shredder and carefully set it for lowest power.

<Loren? Listen! The sub-visser doesn't know you aren't still a Controller. Take this. Stand behind me, where he can see you when I switch on my screen. Give me a few seconds to talk, then fire this. But miss me, okay?>

"Got it," she said.

I switched on my screen. <So, Sub-Visser Seven. You survived. Too bad.>

<I did survive. But you almost got me there, you really did. And by the way, it's no longer Sub-Visser Seven. I'm the first Yeerk to capture an Andalite body. I have already delivered more intelligence on Andalite fleet deployments than a century of spying could have yielded. So it's not *Sub-Visser* anything anymore. You are addressing *Visser* Thirty-Two.>

<You're still just a slug as far as I'm concerned. You want the Time Matrix?> I asked. <Come and take it from me. I promise you —>

TSSSSEEEEWWWW!

Loren fired the shredder on low power. I jerked suddenly, and slumped forward, turning off the screen as I fell.

I jumped back up.

"You want this back?" Loren asked, holding the shredder toward me.

<No. Keep it. You did well. Perfect timing. The visser will think you're still a Controller. He'll think you stunned me. I'm killing all power. We'll just wait for the sub-visser to come to us.>

"Is this going to work?" Loren asked anxiously.

<If it doesn't, neither of us is going to the Yosemite,> I said.

"You picked a great time to learn how to joke, Elfangor."

We didn't have to wait long. The Blade ship fired up its engines and leaped forward. It ate up the few thousand miles in seconds.

<Come to me, Visser whatever-your-number-is-now. Come to me,> I muttered to myself.

I targeted the shredders on the belly of the Blade ship. I was perfectly calm. Despite the battle I knew was raging around the *StarSword*. Despite the approach of the visser's ship. One shot was all I needed. I would wait till he was practically on me. And then —

WHAPPP!

"Ahhhh!"

Chapman! He had freed his legs and kicked Loren's feet. She went down hard. The shredder skittered across the floor.

The human was slower than me. But he was closer. His bound hands closed around the shredder seconds before I reached him.

TSSEEEEEWW!

He fired!

I dodged.

The Blade ship closed in.

TSSEEEEWWW!

<Arrrrggghhh!> A glancing hit. The beam struck my left arm and left foreleg. Pain shot through me

like shards of glass. My left arm was as numb as stone. My left front leg was useless. I could stand, but I could barely move.

"How do you like it, Andalite?" Chapman crowed as he rose to a standing position. He leveled the shredder at me.

"Oh, I have so *had* it with you!" Loren yelled. Still lying on the deck, she drew her legs up and kicked upward. Both her artificial hooves hit Chapman right where his legs joined his body.

"Oooooffff!" Chapman gasped. He grabbed himself with both hands, still clutching the shredder.

I believe the kick was painful to him.

"Oof *this*!" Loren said. She jumped up off the deck and delivered an impossibly high kick that caught Chapman under the chin. His head snapped back. Loren snatched the shredder from him.

"You know, Chapman, you are really making the human race look bad," she said. "You are seriously embarrassing me."

"Who's side are you *on*?" Chapman grated.

"Not yours," Loren said. She fired the shredder and Chapman jerked and went limp.

BUMP! BUMP!

The *Jahar* shook from a slow impact. The Blade ship had latched on! They were boarding us!

As I watched, half-paralyzed, the hatch began to open.

chapter 16

The hatch opened.

<Loren! The shredder. . . . Shoot!>

The hatch door flew open with a boom. Loren fired!

TSSSEEEEWWW!

A Hork-Bajir warrior fell back. An arm appeared, reaching past the collapsed Controller and aiming a Dracon beam.

An Andalite arm!

TSSSSEEEEWWWW!

The Dracon beam fired. The shot missed me but hit Loren and knocked her, already unconscious, into me. With only three good legs, I fell hard to the deck on my numb arm. Loren landed on top of me.

The evil Yeerk creature who had stolen Alloran's body pushed past the Hork-Bajir as I struggled desperately to get out from under Loren.

The visser was in! He was aboard the *Jahar*!

I had one chance. One. And then let the Yeerk kill me! I swung my tail, aiming blind. The visser jerked back reflexively. But I wasn't aiming for him.

The tip of my blade hit the console. And to my great pleasure I heard —

TSSSSWWWWEEEWW!

The *Jahar* fired her shredders. Point-blank range. Point-blank range into the belly of the Blade ship.

<Noooooo!> the visser screamed.

Kuh-BOOOOOOOM! The Blade ship tore loose of the *Jahar.*

FWWOOOOOOSSSH! The hatch was open to space. Air blew from the ship, sending it into a spin. Everything that wasn't bolted down flew toward the open hatch.

The unconscious Hork-Bajir was thrown into space. Chapman's unconscious body slid toward the opening. The visser was knocked down.

But even as he lay there, the Yeerk visser aimed his Dracon beam at me. <You're a real source of agitation, Elfangor. Now, die!>

In despair I whipped my tail.

WHUMPF! Something hit us hard, just as the Yeerk squeezed the trigger.

TSSEEEFWWW! The Dracon blast missed me!

I was gasping for air. The oxygen was gone. The *Jahar* was spinning out of control through space.

The visser slammed against the walls as we spun wildly. Loren's body rolled away toward the hatch, but now the automatic safety devices of the ship were slowly closing the door.

We spun, and through the window I saw flashes of Andalite fighters half-covered with living rock. And Yeerk Bug fighters now suffering the same fate.

I saw, in a wild, spinning flash, the Blade ship, one blade shot away.

And then . . . coming at us . . . rushing toward us . . . an asteroid!

FFWWWUUUMMMPPP!

The asteroid latched onto the poor, dying *Jahar*. And in wild, crazily pitching flashes as I was tossed helplessly, I saw the window going dark. Half-covered now. Half-covered by living rock!

The asteroid had us!

I was slammed violently by acceleration as the asteroid moved away from the battlefield, holding the *Jahar* in its death grip.

The *Jahar*'s compensators were off now. The ship was dead. Half-swooning from lack of air, I staggered up, fighting the insane force of acceleration.

Air! We needed air!

The emergency environmental power unit should have come on. But the ship's power was dead, drained away by the energy-eating asteroid.

Air!

My lungs screamed. My hearts hammered madly, circulating useless blood. The manual emergency tanks, I had to . . . to . . .

But maybe it didn't matter. . . . Maybe it was pointless to fight. Arbron . . . gone. Alloran . . . worse than gone. Terrible things . . . terrible sights . . .

Let it all end. It was fine without air. Fine to suck with your lungs and feel nothing. I was sinking, down, down, down.

No need to worry. Nothing to be afraid of.

Let it end, Elfangor.

Just let it end. . . .

Don't miss
the
andalite
chronicles

#3 An Alien Dies

Visser Thirty-two stood on the bank of the pool in the Yeerk zone, under his own green sky.

And on either side of him stood a creature like nothing I had ever seen or imagined. They were each about three feet tall and four and a half feet long. They were mostly a dark, dirty yellow with irregular black spots. But the head and shoulders were the deep red of the Yeerk plants.

The heads were tiny for the bodies, elongated, almost needle-sharp. The mouths were long and narrow. Hundreds of tiny, bright red teeth stuck out, jagged and wildly different in length and shape.

But what struck me as strangest was that the creatures did not have legs in the usual sense. They had wheels.

Yes, wheels. Four of them, to be exact.

The wheels were located where legs should be. Each was sloppy and irregular in shape, not perfectly round. But it was easy to see that the wheels were for real. There was mud and dirt all around them, and when I strained my stalk eyes I could even see where the creatures had left tracks in the dirt. Wheel tracks.

"Elfangor, what are those things?"

<I have no idea. I can't imagine what evolutionary path would conceivably have created a creature with wheels.>

Visser Thirty-two actually gave a jaunty wave of his hand. <So, young Elfangor, we meet again. As you see, I brought my pets: Jarex and Larex. And you brought your pet, too. Your pet human.>

Loren looked at me. In a voice Visser Thirty-two was sure to hear, she muttered, "You know, Elfangor, I'm beginning to see why you Andalites really dislike Yeerks. Whatever body they may be in, they still have the manner of slugs."

<Brave little human girl,> the Yeerk visser mocked. <Do you understand that even now my people are on their way to evaluate your primitive world? Do you understand that within a few years your people, you humans, will be slaves of the Yeerk Empire?>

"Blah, blah, blah," Loren said.

I had no idea what that meant. Neither did the visser.

"You do a lot of talking for a slug," Loren clarified. "You think I'm scared of you?"

<Yes. I know you're scared of me.>

For a moment Loren said nothing, but her lower lip was trembling slightly. Then, she knelt quickly, plunged her hand into the water and withdrew it. She was holding a rock. She drew her arm back, swept her arm in a big loop and released the rock with precise timing. The rock flew through the air at an impressive speed.

And the aim wasn't bad, either.

BONK!

<Ahhh!> the visser cried. The rock had struck him right in the face, just below his left main eye.

I don't know who was more amazed, me or the visser.

<What . . . what do you call that?> I asked her.

"That? We call that softball. I pitch for Frank's Pro Shop Twins back home. All-city two years in a row."

<What is softball?>

"It's a game we play."

<And you hit people in the face with rocks?>

"Not usually."

I was impressed by the human ability to throw things with such force. I was sure that Andalite scientists would enjoy studying humans some day. They appeared more frail and ridiculous than they were.

The visser was not impressed. He was just angry.

<So. You propel rocks at me! You'll be very sorry you ever propelled a rock at me, human. Jarex! Larex! Attack!>

The situation stopped being amusing very quickly. The twin beasts turned their wheels, sluggishly at first. But then picked up speed.

I almost didn't move, I was so fascinated seeing the biological wheels turn. It was truly incredible.

<You admire my pets, Andalite? They are a species called Mortrons. As a young lieutenant I went on a survey party to a world that was later destroyed when its sun went nova. We thought we might be able to make Controllers of these Mortrons, but that didn't work out. Their brains are simply too tiny to accommodate us. Instead, I brought two of them home as pets.>

All the while the visser talked — or "blah, blah, blahed," as Loren had said — the Mortrons gathered speed and raced around the circumference of the pool.

They made a strange sound. A HUF-HUF-HUF-HUF. Faster and faster.

<They have amazing capacities, my young friend Elfangor. As you will soon see.>

<What's the matter, Yeerk? Afraid to fight me tail-to-tail?> I taunted. I hoped the answer was yes, because I was not at all sure which of us would win a tail fight. While I *was* totally confident I could deal with these Mortrons.

HUF-HUF-HUF-HUF-HUF!

The wheels spun faster, and the ungainly yellow and black monstrosities were nearly to the edge of the Yeerk portion of the pool. I watched carefully to see whether they could move from the Yeerk area into the human area.

Unfortunately, the answer was yes.

<Don't worry,> I told Loren. <I can handle these two creatures.>

HUF-HUF-HUF-HUF-SCRINK-SHWOOOP!

Suddenly the creatures each split into two parts! The bottom portion, the yellow part with the wheels, swerved away. The dark red upper portion simply rose from the body, unfolded leathery wings I'd never even suspected, and flew straight at me!

"Elfangor!" Loren cried.

<Hah-hah! Kill, Jarex! Kill, Larex! Kill the Andalite!> Visser Thirty-two cackled gleefully.

The first Mortron — I don't know if it was Jarex or Larex — opened its mouth and showed its rows of uneven but brutally unpleasant teeth. It powered through the air like a rocket.

I dodged left and struck with my tail blade!

FWAPP!

SPLEET! FLUMP. FLUMP.

My tail blade sliced the Mortron into two chunks. The two separate pieces fell to the ground with a wet splat.

"Elfangor, the other one!"

The second Mortron used the distraction provided by his brother to swoop wide, then arch in behind me. A tactic that would have worked on most opponents. But not on an Andalite who can see in all directions at once.

His toothy mouth was inches from my neck when I struck.

FWAPP!

SPLEET! FLUMP. FLUMP.

And the second Mortron bird-portion fell in pieces to the ground.

I was feeling pretty good, until I looked at the visser and saw the amusement in his eyes.

"Elfangor, look. Look!" Loren cried.

I turned my stalk eyes toward the ground. With amazing speed, the two bloody halves of each Mortron were growing. One piece of each was growing to become a complete bird-portion again. And the other piece was going even further — growing into a complete, two-piece, yellow and black, four-wheeled Mortron.

I had sliced both Mortrons in half. And now they were becoming four Mortrons.

<Are you doing the math in your head, Elfangor?> the visser jeered. <They regenerate! Cut an attacking Mortron in pieces and each piece grows again to become a complete Mortron. It's the killing frenzy. It gives them an enzyme boost that makes them regenerate! Try to kill these four and you'll have eight. Kill those eight and you'll have sixteen! Thirty-two! Sixty-four!>

I stared in horror as the Mortron pieces grew and grew. In seconds they would be ready to attack again. And anything I did to destroy them would merely make more of them!

<Loren, I don't know what to do. If only I had a shredder!>

"Can you outrun them?"

<Yes, I can. But you can't! They are faster than you are. And I won't leave you.>

"You won't have to. Maybe. How strong is your back? Never mind, it must be strong enough. Elfangor, don't be offended, okay?"

<Offended by what?>

"Hold still. I'm gonna try something."

She came to me and placed one hand on the back of my neck. She placed another hand on my rump, right at the base of my tail. And suddenly, she leaned her weight on me, swung one leg up and over, and came to rest straddling my back. She sat there with one human leg hanging off either side of my back and held her hands clasped around my neck.

I turned my stalk eyes around and found myself staring directly into her small blue human eyes.

"Now let's run," she said.

<With you on my back?>

But even while I was standing there in blank astonishment, I saw a fully-formed Mortron rise from the dirt. It was just a few feet away and it launched its bird-part. Leather wings propelled jagged razor-sharp teeth straight for my throat.

"Elfangor, this is not the time to think," Loren yelled. "Run! Ruuuuun!"

So I did. With the human girl actually on my back, I ran.